LUCY OF LARKHILL

Lucy Wells is left to run her Dartmoor farm virtually on her own after a hired hand is injured. She does her best to carry on; though when she decides to sell her baked goods direct to the public, she is forced to admit that she is overwhelmed. She needs to hire a man to help on the farm, and her childhood friend Stephen might just be the answer. But as Lucy's feelings for him grow, she is more determined than ever to remain an independent spinster . . .

CHRISTINA GREEN

◆

LUCY OF LARKHILL

Complete and Unabridged

LINFORD
Leicester

First published in Great Britain in 2015

First Linford Edition
published 2016

A catalogue record for this book is available
from the British Library.

ISBN 978–1–4448–2874–0

Published by
F. A. Thorpe (Publishing)
Anstey, Leicestershire

Set by Words & Graphics Ltd.
Anstey, Leicestershire
Printed and bound in Great Britain by
T. J. International Ltd., Padstow, Cornwall

This book is printed on acid-free paper

1

I stood in the doorway of the farm-house, watching as the wedding guests threw rice and complimentary remarks at Peter, my brother, and his lovely bride, Annie. How handsome they looked, Pete wearing the specially bought dark suit and carrying the grey top hat that Annie had insisted he wear, despite his mutterings about this being a new century so why go back into the Victorian past? And Annie looked a picture, small and sparkling, in her going-away blue crêpe walking costume.

Pete hugged me. 'Lucy, I hate leaving you like this, but we shan't be far away. I'll always come if you need me.'

His eyes stared lovingly into mine and somehow I kept the tears at bay, forcing my voice to be light. 'Don't worry about me, Pete! I'll manage all right — after all, I've got Mike and old

Joe to help, haven't I? And I'm not just a pretty face, you know. I'm strong and capable. And I've worked on this farm all my life, remember!'

Then Annie was at my side, arms around me, her warmth giving me new strength as she said quietly, 'Of course you'll manage, Lucy. But come and see us when you can. We shall only be an hour's drive away in the trap, you know.'

I nodded. 'Perhaps on a Sunday afternoon, if I can get Joe to come in and milk the cow. Now off you go, Annie, and enjoy your honeymoon. Thank goodness the sun is still shining!'

Goodbyes are horrible, and this one was particularly so, for Pete and I had been running Larkhill Farm together since Father had died some five years ago. And now I would be alone.

But I pushed aside the anxious thoughts, watching as they climbed into the newly painted gig lent by our neighbour, Will Neal. Pete clucked to the pony and off they went, portmanteau, valises and hat-boxes rattling as the cart drove over the cobbles, out of the farm entrance and down the lane.

Thank goodness, I thought, for those friends waving and cheering and still throwing rice. What a wedding it had been! And the wedding feast had been so successful, with all my pastries, pies, puddings and cakes, and homemade cider going down a treat. Only a few crumbs were left on the long table in the kitchen. But now for the clearing up, I told myself wryly as I turned back to the house and went inside. There were enough bits and pieces left over to keep me going for a day or so — and no doubt good old Mrs. Yeo next door would come and help me.

Then something brushed against my knee and I looked down. It was Fly, my dear old sheepdog, always my companion and workmate. I pushed aside my fears and patted his grey head. 'All right, Fly,' I said, smiling. 'We'll face it together, won't we, boy?'

I set myself to a more positive frame of mind. There was the usual work to be done: milking Daisy, collecting eggs, checking on the sheep before nightfall, and finally shutting up the hens. I had given Mike and Joe the rest of the day off, so these jobs were all waiting for me; and already I could hear Daisy wandering back into the cowshed, telling me it was high time for milking.

But before that I must change out of this elegant new dark green dress with its lighter braiding, high lace collar and tight sleeves, to say nothing of the large flower-bedecked hat that Annie had chosen, saying it suited me and looked lovely. I went up to my bedroom under the eaves, changing into my usual working clothes: the old woollen skirt, which never showed the dirt; a faded blouse; and lastly a shawl around my shoulders — for Dartmoor gets chilly as evenings close in.

It had been strange going into the village and finding a new dress, for smart clothes don't come naturally into farming life. Now I put the dress carefully into the big mahogany wardrobe, thinking it most unlikely that I would ever wear it again. But it would hang there safely, just in case. After all, one never knew what life would bring, did one?

For a second, marriage flashed through my mind, but I dismissed it. I would stay here at Larkhill, working my farm and growing into an eccentric old maid. Who would want to marry a workaday girl like me, anyway? I had none of Annie's prettiness; just a strong mind and equally strong arms and legs. No, I was content to carry on as I was.

I made my way out into the fresh air and took a quick look around as I headed for the cowshed. Dartmoor has wide skies, and the sunset was already spreading out its fiery colours. A small line of threatening grey clouds ranged up from the west, and I guessed the weather was due for a change.

Summer sunshine is lovely, but rain is what is needed to help things grow, and farming relies on the weather being kind. Again, I was grateful for today's perfect warmth and cloudless skies for the wedding. When I returned to the house, jobs done and a basket of eggs to be washed and put ready for sale at market, I found Mrs. Yeo waiting for me, her grey hair neatly pulled back into a bun with a crisp white cap perched on top of it. She nodded her head and smiled.

'What a grand day, my lover! Those two all nicely all done up and having a good send-off, and now you and me to clear up the mess! Thought I'd come in now, not leave it till tomorrow.'

I was so glad to see her. I'd been afraid the house would seem too empty without Pete, and with Mike spending the evening down in the village, but now I had company for a while.

'Very good of you to come, Mrs. Yeo. Let's have a cup before we start work, shall we?'

We put the old black kettle back on the hot range and I found a couple of clean mugs. I cut a big slice of the remains of the wedding cake and put it in front of her, saying, 'Because you're such a good and kind neighbour, Mrs. Yeo, and I hope you enjoy it. One of my ma's old recipes.'

She munched in silence for a minute or two, then said, 'Really good, Lucy. You and your cakes. I see them on sale in the shop — selling well, I reckon?'

'Yes,' I said, making the tea and smiling at her. 'But I don't suppose I shall have time to do much baking now that I'm alone here — ' I stopped sharply, for the words came out without thinking, and I heard them echoing around my mind.

Mrs. Yeo put out her wrinkled hand and touched my arm. 'You'll manage, maid. Big strong girl like you — and you got young Mike and Joe to help.'

I banished the anxiety and nodded. 'Yes, you're right. And it's good that Pete and Annie are taking over her father's farm — why, electricity has been installed in the kitchen over there, and even running water! No more dragging buckets from the well like we do, and all our dirty old oil lamps to clean every day!'

Mrs. Yeo smiled, but it was a nostalgic expression. 'This new century brings all sort of things, don't it, my lover? Talk of motor cars instead of our pony traps — imagine that!'

'Difficult to,' I said. 'Think I'll stick with the old-fashioned ways as long as I can, even though the work's so hard.'

We exchanged smiles.

'Well, better get on with the clearing up, I suppose, now we've finished our tea. Let's put all the eatables in the larder, then we'll collect up the plates and mugs. Ready, Mrs. Yeo?'

It was late and getting really dark by the time we'd finished clearing up, and Mike appeared, home from his evening in the village. He was a good boy, an apprentice taken on by my father several years before he died, and now part of our family and our farm. The workhouse must have been hard for a child, so I allowed him more freedom than perhaps many another lad enjoyed working on a farm.

'You look like you need a good night's sleep, Mike. No, don't tell me what you got up to down there. I can guess — admiring girls, and a few mugs of ale! Want anything to eat?'

'No thanks, missus; had a bite at the inn. But yes, I'm ready for me bed.'

He grinned at us, then stomped upstairs and we heard his bedroom door shut. I knew he'd be fine in the morning, and up before I opened my eyes. Again, I thought how lucky I was to have such help; and as I bade Mrs. Yeo goodnight and thanked her, I found I was ready for a little sit-down by the fire before going to bed myself.

As I sat there, drowsy in the warmth, lulled by the whispers from the dying embers, I thought about the gossipy news that she had told me. Stephen Neal was coming home from Australia, where he'd gone after that last awful row with Will, his elder brother. Then happy memories of childhood days came back, of times shared with both the Neal boys as we grew up: football in the field, climbing the tors, running races, damming up rivers, fighting — yes, Will and Stephen had always fought, with me telling them to stop; not to be so stupid. And sometimes getting involved in their arguments, for I had always said what was on my mind.

And now Stephen was coming home. Would he return to the old home farm that Will now worked with Emma, his wife? Would he fit in there if he did so? For village gossip said Emma ran the roost, giving orders and expecting to be obeyed. I frowned, foreseeing more rows — but oh, I did hope not. As I had grown up I had realised that life was so much easier if people got on, understood each other and made allowances. But would Stephen and Will think that way?

I shook my head as I banked up the fire, made sure Fly was safe in his kennel outside, bolted the door, and made my way to bed. Curled up in warm sheets, head on the pillow, I had a few last, sleepy thoughts, hoping Pete and Annie were happy.

And then a shadow crept over everything: I was alone here now. But I forced back the word and slipped into a dreamless sleep that came like a blessing, helping me to be ready for whatever the new day — and my new life — might bring.

⋆　⋆　⋆

Rain lashed at the window as I got up and dressed. I saw Mike, an old sack covering his head and shoulders, running towards the cowshed while Joe stood in the barn doorway, looking up at the racing clouds. Old men like Joe always knew what the weather would do. I grinned as I left the house, pulling Father's old Ulster coat over me.

Joe nodded and said, 'Jest a shower or two, missus. Bright again later. Best you stay in and do yer baking — Mike an' me can manage out here. No need fer all of us to get wet. I'm goin' along with the muck — needs spreadin' in the far field.'

He disappeared and I heard him talking to Duchess, the cart horse, who would pull the cart once it was loaded.

I looked at the sky. Joe was always right; and yes, it would be best for me to stay in and get on with the next batch of cakes for the shop while I had the chance. The owners of the village shop, the Hannaford family, took a weekly box of eggs, some honey when the bees had plenty, and lately a small basket or two of my cakes. And they sold well. I had found Ma's recipe book when we sorted out Father's things, and there were all these old recipes — sponge cakes, gingerbread men, biscuits, seedy cake and tarts, full of either treacle or fresh fruit from our orchard. It seemed a wonderful opportunity to make use of the old ideas and earn some extra pennies.

And Alan Hannaford was very keen for me to carry on baking. Last week he had followed me to the shop door saying, 'When the wedding's over, Lucy, you'll be on your own, won't you? A chance, perhaps, for us to get to know each other a bit better? I know we're friends already, but, well . . .'

His slow, hesitant speech had trailed off, but I saw from the expression in his eyes what he was hoping for, and I knew at once that I must be careful, for I had no wish to be more than a casual friend to Alan. I was already good friends with Lizzie, his sister, which was fine; but anything more wasn't in my scheme of things. I was going to be too busy to think about Alan's hopes. So I had smiled hastily and backed out of the door.

'Nice of you, Alan, but I shall have lots more work to do now Pete's gone, so shan't really have any time to spare.' And I'd made a quick retreat round the corner and up the hill back to Larkhill.

Later that afternoon, Lizzie came to call. As usual, she was wearing a bright ribbon round her hat, and her coat had patches sewn over the most worn bits. Her red hair shone in the sun and I was glad to see her, for she always cheered me up.

'Well, Lucy,' she said, pulling a stool from under the table and sitting down, 'I hope you're making some more cakes — they sell well. But what I've come to tell you is that there's to be a barn dance next week in the Neals' barn, and of course we must go.'

I put the pie I was making for our tea into the oven, wiped flour off my arms and sat down opposite her, my face glowing with the heat from the fire. 'Barn dance? Oh, I don't think I've got the energy, Lizzie — all this extra work I'm doing.'

Lizzie gave one of her noisy guffaws. 'Of course you'll come. I'm not going on my own, and Alan has two left feet, so he's no good to dance with! No, you an' me'll go together and, tell you what, we must dress up to look especially pretty!'

Her smile was wicked and my

interest was caught. 'Why, for goodness sake?'

'Cos there's going to be a special person there, that's why. You must know that Stephen Neal's coming back from Australia? If you don't you must be the only girl in the village not to know! But he's sure to be there at the barn dance, so don't say you won't come now!'

2

That, of course, was food for thought for a few minutes, while Lizzie chattered on about how she was making herself a new skirt with which to gather admiring eyes at the barn dance.

I knew how clever she was with her needle, so I showed some interest, asking, 'What colour?'

'Brown and green check, a bit of cotton I found at Moreton market last week. Oh yes, it'll look good — very full, so that it twirls round when I spin like this!' She jumped to her feet and showed me exactly how she would spin, sending all the flour flying over the table.

'Lizzie,' I cried, 'just sit down and keep still, can't you? Look at all this mess! But go on, tell me what you'll wear on top of this wonderful skirt.'

She sank down on the stool again,

looking apologetic. 'Sorry, Lucy, but I'm so excited about the barn dance. I shall wear my old white shirt with a bit of lace round the collar. I want to look nice, you see.'

I envied her a bit. 'And why must you look so nice, I wonder?' I asked, wiping my hands and pulling the kettle over the fire to make us a drink.

She gave me a saucy look and I had a feeling that I wasn't going to like what she told me. I didn't, as she replied, 'Why, because Stephen will be there of course, and I'm going to make sure he dances with me!'

I turned round to hide my expression, spooning tea into the teapot. Why did I feel like this? After all, Lizzie had every right to admire Stephen, as did any other girl in the village. Yet somehow I felt he was my particular friend, not belonging to anyone else.

I busied myself finding mugs and pouring tea. Something knotted inside me. Just because Stephen and I had been friends several years ago, there was no reason to think either of us would want to renew that friendship. And yet, as I half-listened to Lizzie burbling on about using a strip of the skirt material to make a bow for her hair, the truth hit me. He had once been my good friend, and now I needed that friendship again. But would he feel the same as me?

Lizzie and I drank our tea and then she skipped out of the door, calling back, 'See you on Friday next week — and wear something pretty, for goodness sake!'

★   ★   ★

I spent the evening sorting out old clothes — even some of Ma's, stored long ago under the bed. They were flimsy and a bit mouldy, but among them was a lovely taffeta skirt of dark blue that still held its elegance and cleanliness. Holding it up and looking in the mirror, I found it fitted me — perhaps an inch to be taken in at the waist. But how good it would look with the blue-grey silk blouse I had bought in a village jumble sale and had never had a chance to wear. I thought it was a cast-off from the ladies who once lived at the Manor; such lovely rich material and subtle colour. And now, I thought, tidying my hair back into a neat roll around my head and securing it with pins, the skirt and blouse would come into their own. Lizzie might look pretty in her bright colours, but I too, would have reason to catch eyes, wouldn't I?

Hanging up the skirt to give it a good airing, I wondered just whose eyes I planned to catch. My dreams that night didn't reveal anyone in particular, but I was smiling when I awoke.

And then life played one of its tricks. Mike ran into the kitchen, looking anxious. 'I'd better go and see where Joe is, missus,' he said. 'No sign of him yet, an' he's never late, is he?'

No, I thought, alarmed. Never one single day had he been late, not in all the years he'd worked at Larkhill.

19

Something must be wrong. 'Go and see what's happening, Mike,' I said. 'I'll do the milking, but hurry back.'

He went off at a dash. I put on my old apron and battered felt hat and went to the cowshed to milk Daisy. On my way, I thought how childish and silly I had been yesterday with all that fuss about dressing up for a barn dance, when real life was far more important. Suppose Joe was ill, or hurt? Ideas gathered and I frowned as I carried the bucket of milk back to the cooler outside the kitchen door.

I was still there when Mike returned, standing in front of me, his ruddy face a bit pale and his voice unusually quiet. 'He's broke his leg, missus. Fell down the last two steps — you know how dark that old cottage is, and I s'ppose his rheumatics made him wobble a bit. But the doctor's there; says he gotta go to hospital to have his leg strapped up and get over the shock of the fall. Poor ol' Mrs. Joe's in a real state, I can tell you.'

We stared at each other for a long moment until I said, 'I'll go and see her. And you and me, Mike — well, we'll have to do the work until Joe gets better.'

He was silent for a bit, then nodded and said stoutly, 'You can depend on me, missus. I'll do the best I can. You and Mr. Pete've always been good to me, so now I can repay you.'

I swallowed the lump in my throat, saying unsteadily, 'Thanks, Mike, that's wonderful. We'll get by — somehow.'

Then I went into the house to collect my purse and jacket before making my way to Joe's cottage at the far end of the village. Yes, I had told Mike we would manage, but my thoughts were confused and unhappy as I turned in at Joe's white-painted garden gate.

Biddy, Joe's wife, met me in the doorway, her lined face pale and her hands trembling as she reached out to hold mine. 'Those ol' stairs! Always telling him to watch out in the dark, weren't I, but he never listened and

21

now — oh my soul, what'll we do, Miss Lucy? My Joe taken off to Moreton hospital in the doctor's carriage, and how'll I get there to see him, take him his clothes and razor and things?'

Her voice was unsteady, and I guided her to the kitchen and a chair by the fire. 'Don't worry, Biddy,' I said as calmly as I could. 'I'll take you into Moreton this afternoon, and I expect Joe will come home once he's strapped up.' But I feared it was more than likely to be a long stay in hospital for Joe, although of course I didn't say so.

I smiled and suggested, 'How about a cup of tea? Cheer us up, wouldn't it?' I pushed the singing kettle closer over the heat.

A little colour seeped back into her cheeks, and her voice was more even as she said, 'Good of you, Miss Lucy. Thank you. But what about the work? And with Mr. Pete gone you're on your own, and no Joe — oh dear, what a muddle it all is.'

I said firmly, 'Don't worry about the

work; Mike and I can manage. He's a good boy, very willing — and if necessary I can get someone from the village till Joe's ready to come back.'

But even as I said it, I had a feeling that Joe would never return to Larkhill. Ageing, rheumatics worsening, and now a broken leg. Waiting for the kettle to boil, my thoughts ran in circles. Of course Mike and I couldn't manage on our own. But who among the village men, already busy with their own work, could I ask to come and help out? And then the kettle spluttered all over the hob and I had to make a dash for the teapot.

We drank our cups of strong tea, and gradually Biddy grew less anxious. I left her eventually, saying, 'I'll bring the trap round after dinner, if you'll be ready. You can spend a bit of time with Joe while I pick up some shopping, and then . . . ' I paused, remembering that their daughter, married to a baker, lived in the village. 'Perhaps Martha — ?'

She picked up my thoughts at once. Her smile broadened. 'Of course, I'll go to Martha. She'll want to know about her pa, and I can stay there for a while.' She got to her feet. 'I'll be ready when you come — my, but you be a proper angel, Miss Lucy. An' now I'll go and get some things together — his razor, clean clothes, my nightie . . .'

I watched her climb the narrow, creaking stairs and then I walked back to Larkhill. There were many jobs to do before I harnessed Duchess in the trap and set off on our afternoon journey.

Moreton was quiet, this not being a market day, and I reached the hospital in good time for visiting. I left Biddy with her bags and parcels and even a smile on her face as she said goodbye.

I had a couple of errands to do, so left Duchess and the trap in the square and went quickly around the shops. Candles and — I paused outside the haberdasher's — perhaps something to tie up my hair ready for the barn dance? Lizzie's words echoed around my mind as I went inside. I hardly ever spent money on myself, and ribbon didn't cost much. I picked a length of dark blue satin and was coming out of the shop, ready to return to the square and drive home, when a gig whirled down the street beside me, the woman driver shouting back over her shoulder.

'You'll have to walk. I can't wait any longer.' Then the gig disappeared round the corner in a flurry of dust. I knew who it was: Emma Neal, Will's high-and-mighty wife. Amused, I wondered who she'd been shouting at.

As I reached Duchess and the trap, another voice sounded behind me — a voice I remembered, calling my name. I caught my breath. Surely it couldn't be — ?

'Lucy! Lucy Wells!'

I turned and looked into Stephen Neal's face. I just stood there like a breathless idiot, thinking to myself that he hadn't changed. That suntanned face, the charm already reaching me and making me smile. Perhaps he was a bit older, more lined, the lantern jaw looking even stronger than I remembered — but goodness, still so handsome. Still my friend, was he?

No words came to me. I held out my hand and felt pleasure filling me, but I waited to hear his voice again.

'Lucy Wells! What a nice surprise.' He took my hand and at last words stumbled out.

'So good to see you again, Stephen. I heard you were coming back, but I didn't know . . . '

He grinned. 'Heard the village gossip, did you?'

'Of course, but no details. Have you and Will made up your differences? Are you staying with him and Emma?' As usual, I said everything that was in my mind, and he chuckled as if he, too, recognised something about me that hadn't changed, despite the years gone by.

'Just the same, aren't you, Lucy? Still saying just what you think. Yes, I'm staying at Hayes Farm for a while, until I find myself somewhere else. And no, Will and I are still arguing.'

I wanted to ask about Emma but stopped just in time. I really must learn to be more tactful. So I said, more quietly, 'Well, if you'd like to call in at Larkhill, Mike and I'll be glad to see you.'

'What about Pete? I heard he's married and moved away. You must miss him.'

'Yes,' I said. 'Of course I'm pleased he and Annie are married. They've moved to Tavistock. And I do miss him. A lot.'

He nodded. 'And Joe? Hope he's still going strong.'

I paused. 'I'm afraid not. Joe's broken his leg and he's in hospital. I'll miss him, too.'

He regarded me for a long moment. 'So you'll need some help, Lucy. Can't manage it all on your own, can you?'

I said brightly, 'Of course I can manage. I'm used to hard work. Now you probably want a lift back to the village, don't you? I heard Emma shouting at you as she drove off. How are you getting on with her?'

I knew immediately I shouldn't have asked. He frowned, the lines round his eyes crinkling, reminding me how strong and determined he had always been. 'Emma's not keen to have me around the farm, and I don't blame her. Why should she have a returned brother-in-law filling up her house and arguing with her husband? I shall move on soon as I can.'

We looked at each other. I nodded, then said quickly, 'Jump in then, and we'll drive back to the village. I've got plenty to do back at Larkhill.'

We didn't speak as I drove back down the twisting lanes. I guessed that like me, he was enjoying the greenery of the sprouting hedges and the hazy distant tors with the sun gleaming on them. Different from Australia, I thought, and wanted to ask him, but something stopped me. Stephen was clearly planning a new life for himself, and if he could just stay my friend then I'd be satisfied.

He jumped out of the trap as I drew up in the farm yard, and gave me one of his big smiles. As he turned away, he said over his shoulder, 'Thanks for the lift, Lucy. See you around, I expect.' And then he was gone, striding down the road, leaving me feeling more alone than ever.

3

The days rushed past. So much work, so little time. I was tired out by the evening and simply ready for a meal by the fire, with Mike whittling away at the bit of wood that he said would one day be a model sailing ship. We chatted about the farm and about the work, which seemed to be getting heavier and more difficult.

It was an evening such as this when Mike asked me, reluctantly I thought, 'Your cattle up the hill, missus — they've pushed one of the newtake walls about, so they'm getting out of the Larkhill land. I tried to get 'em back, but it's too hard. I need someone to help there, missus.'

I came out of my dream of a handyman from the village looking for work. 'The walls? Mike, you should have told me before. I'll go up there tomorrow and see what's to be done.'

'You can't do it alone, missus. Needs someone strong to get those old stones up again.' He put down the wooden carving and looked at me anxiously. 'Ol' Joe an' I were gonna do it, but now . . . well.' He shook his head.

So, another job for tomorrow: ride out and look at the cattle, and then decide what to do about the broken walls. I sighed and decided today had enough problems. Perhaps sleep would help me deal with the even bigger one tomorrow.

'Bed,' I said, getting up. 'Put away your woodwork, Mike. We'll go straight out after breakfast. Baking will have to wait.' But I knew it couldn't. The shop had already sold out of the last batch of cakes, and Alan was demanding another lot. Perhaps if I stayed up all night?

I went upstairs chuckling, because it seemed the only thing to do. Better than worrying and not sleeping. Determination grew as I took off my clothes; somehow I would get those walls up again and my cattle on their proper land.

★ ★ ★

The morning was blowy but fine. Small clouds raced across the vast blue sky, and the granite tors shone like icicles beneath the radiant sunlight. I was glad to tack up Duchess and head her for the moorland above the farm. She skittered as we rode up the hill, and I felt her pleasure at being free of the restraining trap and cart for once.

Mike had gone on ahead with his bag of tools, and I allowed myself to rest for a few calm moments when we reached the hilltop and saw the moor stretching away into the distance. The view was wonderful: green slopes, glittering stones, and down in the valley the gleam of the river flowing along. And there, high above, circling up, up into the blue, spiraled a skylark, singing its paean of praise. I felt the thrill of its silvery song running down through my body as the memories came

32

to me. I might have been up here, years ago, with Pa and Pete. I loved Dartmoor, and felt once more such gratitude for being born here, part of Larkhill Farm. I would never leave it, I knew — it was the one place that I wanted to live — so somehow I had to cope with all the never-ending work.

My mind returned to Stephen. Was this how he felt about Dartmoor? Was it why he had come home? But Mike was now in sight, so I put aside all thoughts save what to do about the newtake walls containing the Larkhill land.

They certainly looked the worse for wear. I remembered Pete and my father years ago working on those same stones, but now weather and age had caused them to crumble and fall in places. Those were the spots where my cattle could ease through and leave Larkhill, to wander wherever they liked, and be very difficult to round up and bring home again. Definitely the walls needed shoring up, and at once — but who was to do it?

Mike threw down the stone he was trying to heave back into place as I rode up. 'Can't do it alone,' he said, and I nodded. Of course he couldn't. He needed a man's help. My brain was working overtime — and then suddenly an idea flashed in. Why not ask Stephen Neal if he had a few days to spare? He obviously wasn't working at the moment, and perhaps he might be glad to be up here in the sun, on the shining moorland, putting the old walls to rights. And he had asked if I needed help. It was important to get the job done, so I decided to ask him. He could only say no, and then I would have to look elsewhere. But perhaps . . .

I told Mike to leave the work and come back to Larkhill, where there were plenty of other things waiting to be done. But I didn't say anything about Stephen. 'I'll find someone in the village,' I said, turning Duchess and preparing to ride home. 'Maybe someone will be glad to have a few days' work,' I added.

I don't know why I hadn't mentioned Stephen; was it because my mind was too full of him? I shook my head to clear it and headed down the hill without waiting for Mike's answer.

Back at Larkhill, I continued riding down to the village, knowing that I must see Stephen before nerves got the better of me. I rode to Hayes Farm and saw Will in the distance. He waved and shouted, 'Emma's in the kitchen. I'll be in directly — go on in, Lucy.'

But I didn't go in; I was afraid Emma would say something unkind about Stephen, and I didn't want to get involved in family rows. So I looked around me, hoping that Stephen was about and that I could have a quiet word with him. But Emma had heard Will shouting, and there she was at the kitchen door, looking at me with her penetrating green eyes.

'Morning, Lucy. Come in. I want to ask you about cakes for the barn dance on Friday.' She disappeared, and I knew I had to do as she wanted. Tying

Duchess to a hook in the wall, I followed Emma into the farmhouse and found her in the kitchen, cracking eggs into a big bowl. She nodded at a chair and went on stirring.

'I'm not a cook like you. Will says he married the wrong woman!' She grinned, but I heard a hardness in her voice. 'How long do I have to keep doing this?'

'Give it to me. Just get them nice and light.' I whipped the eggs for a minute or two and then handed the bowl back. 'What about the barn dance?' I prompted, glad to change the subject.

She pushed the bowl aside and sat down. 'We want lots of small cakes, some pies, and what about jam tarts? Easy things to pick up and eat while you're jigging about! Will's got the cider barrel all ready, and the hay bales are in place, so it's just the food — and I can't manage it. Will you help?'

'Of course I will, Emma. Glad to be useful. I'll get baking this afternoon. But at the moment, I was hoping to have a word with Stephen.'

I didn't like the way she was looking at me; I wondered if those keen eyes could read my mind. 'Stephen? What do you want him for? He's around somewhere, being of no help to Will, I bet. And of course he expects to live with us — for how long, I wonder?' Her voice was tight and I could see from her expression that her temper was rising.

As lightly as possible, I said, 'Well, I might just have a job or two for him, if he's interested.' Then I stopped, for she looked at me as if I'd said something really terrible.

'Oh,' she said slowly, 'like that, is it? You want Stephen to come up to Larkhill, do you? Well, I never thought you'd throw your feelings about, Lucy Wells. Always thought you a strong sort of maid. But there, you're getting on a bit now, aren't you? And I suppose Stephen would do as well as anybody if you really want a husband.'

We stared at each other, and I could think of nothing to say, so shocked was

I at her turn of thought. And then the door opened and Stephen came in. He looked at us and smiled warily.

'What's this, a cookery lesson for Emma?'

'No,' I said, quickly, 'just talking about the food for the barn dance on Friday.'

He pulled a stool from under the table and sat down beside me. 'Lucy, I've got a sort of proposition for you — could we have a talk about it, say this afternoon?'

Before I could reply Emma was on her feet, pulling the humming kettle towards her and reaching for the tea caddy. 'Goodness, not a proposal, is it, Stephen? I bet she'll say yes!' Her gleaming green eyes dared me to answer back, and somehow I managed a smile, although my body was tight and anger flared deep inside me.

'That's enough of that, Emma,' I said firmly. 'Yes, I'll be at home baking this afternoon, Stephen. You're welcome to come any time.' I got up, frowned across the table, and said, 'And I'll thank you to mind your own business, Emma Neal. I'll live the life I want without advice from you. And don't forget those eggs — they'll go off quickly in this hot room. But I expect you know that.'

I flounced out of the kitchen and banged the door behind me. I heard Emma shout something, but I wasn't listening. All I could think of was what she had said.

I rode up the hill in a hurry, pushing poor Duchess on, while my mind ran round in circles. How dare she! I mean, as if I did plan to marry — Stephen, or anybody! As we clopped into the yard, I shouted to the bright morning, 'That's the last thing I'll ever do! I don't need a husband.' Then I led Duchess into the stable.

But by the time I went back into the kitchen, I had strange new thoughts that took me to the fireside chair, where I wasted precious time sitting and thinking when I should have been doing a hundred other things.

In the afternoon I was back in the yard, seeing to the new sacks of corn and feed, when Stephen rode in on a beautiful black stallion. I looked up, surprised. 'What a fine horse — not Will's, is he?'

He dismounted and led the horse towards the stable. 'No, he's mine. Can I put him in the spare stall, Lucy, while we talk?' His voice was light but his smile was missing. I wondered if something was wrong — another row with Will, perhaps. I hoped not.

'Yes, of course. And then come into the kitchen.'

I put down the small amount of corn I had doled out, secured the big sack, and then went indoors. I had tidied the kitchen up, trying to come to terms with the nervousness that had filled me since that bother with Emma this morning. What could Stephen want? And where had he got this splendid stallion? I could only wait and wonder.

He came in, suntanned, blond where

the Australian sun had bleached his falling mop of untidy hair — and there was something about him. Stephen had always had a presence, even as a lad, when he was king of the village mischief-makers. Now I felt it more than ever, and so sat down quietly without saying anything. Let him do the talking.

He sat down heavily on the opposite side of the table and stretched out his long legs. 'Lucy, as I said this morning, I have a proposition to put to you.'

I must have moved nervously in my chair, for his smile flowered and he leaned forward. 'Don't look so worried! I've got an idea that just might suit us both.' He paused, and a gentler note came into his voice. 'I know you must be missing Pete, especially now that poor Joe is in hospital. You and that lad Mike can't possibly manage on your own, so I was thinking . . . '

'Yes?' I was almost holding my breath — what could he possibly want?

'I'm willing to help out with anything

41

you can't manage between you. I'd be glad to do so. And I wonder — well, the thing is, Lucy, I need pasture land. And I wondered if, for the time being, I could use yours.'

We stared at each other, and I let out my breath very slowly. 'But Stephen, why do you want land all of a sudden?'

He straightened up. 'That stallion's going to be the start of my stud. I worked with horses in Australia, and I've come back with the hopes of starting a business of my own. My land, my horses.' His eyes glowed and his powerful hands were fists on his chair arm. So he had a dream of running his own farm; of not having to be beholden to Will and Emma. And he wanted, for the time being, until he could buy his own land, to use Larkhill. My Larkhill.

There was something about his manner that niggled, but I smiled at him as I answered. 'Larkhill isn't very big, as you probably remember. But there's room for a horse or two to graze until you find your own place. And I should certainly be grateful for your help for a day or so. You see, we're having trouble with the old newtake walls, and Mike can't rebuild them on his own.'

Stephen got up suddenly and paced around the kitchen, clearly intent on sharing his plans with me. 'I hope to find a tenanted farm to start with — not much land, but enough. And then, as they breed, I shall show my beauties.' He nodded, stopped beside my chair, looked down at me, and grinned. His voice grew steely. 'Will won't know what's hit him!'

Dismayed, I realised that Stephen still held on to his animosity, and I didn't like it. But I knew better than to bring it up. This plan would be between Stephen and me, and so it would stay. I took a deep breath, then said calmly, 'Yes, Stephen. If you'll help us with the walls, then I'll be glad to let you graze your stallion on my land — for a while.'

He reached out his hand and offered it to me. I got up and took it in mine. It was powerful, strong, warm, and full of old memories.

'That's settled, then,' I said, and he looked into my eyes as if, like me, he was remembering past days.

I moved away, for it was time to return to reality. 'Now I have to get on with the baking for the barn dance,' I said. 'But if you care to ride your stallion up to the walls, you'll see just what's needed.'

For a moment longer than was necessary he stood still, looking at me. Then he nodded, walked to the door, grinned back at me and said, 'Hope you'll be making a treacle tart. I had dreams about that while I was away . . . ' His voice strengthened. 'Thanks, Lucy. I'll be seeing you again very soon — first thing tomorrow morning, if that's all right?'

I weighed out a mug of sugar and put it into the basin — anything to stop my hands trembling. I looked across the room at him and gave him what I hoped was a friendly but authoritative smile. 'That's fine, Stephen. See you then. Goodbye for now.'

I cut a chunk of butter so that I wouldn't have to look at him anymore. I heard the door latch, his footsteps crunching in the yard, and then his voice, deep and quiet, talking to the stallion as he rode it out of my yard. And then I let out all the breath that I had been holding in my stiff, disturbed body.

4

Somehow the days slipped past: the usual work; the varying weather; repairs to the walls, with Stephen lending his greater weight and expertise to Mike's, so that slowly and with enormous labour the old walls built up again and I felt my stock was safe once more. I kept out of Stephen's way, thinking it best to get on with my own work and let him concentrate on his. But I made a point of riding up every midday and taking them a good bait: pies, cheese, onions, and new bread; and a billycan of tea seemed to give them pleasure and new strength.

I lingered one day, inspecting the walls as they ate the picnic, and was glad to have Stephen come to my side. 'We're doing well. Young Mike's a good boy; he does the best he can. And now, Lucy, have I your permission to let

Apollo loose in these pastures? He's very frustrated at being stuck in Will's stables — and I don't want my first stallion to wear himself out with efforts to escape, do I?'

I turned and met his smiling eyes. 'Yes, bring him up here, Stephen, but do mind he doesn't race off and get stuck in a bog. Do you remember those wicked green feather beds we used to dare each other to put our feet in when we were small?'

He laughed and I did too, for suddenly those past years were very close, bringing back our enjoyment at being on the moor, at daring to try silly tricks, and being such good friends. I saw the expression on his suntanned face and knew I must look the same at this moment. Yes, we had been good friends.

Then Mike shouted that Duchess was getting restless, and the moment was finished. I turned away from Stephen and said over my shoulder, quickly and without any emotion,

'Sorry, have to get home now. The barn dance baking needs finishing.'

I didn't look back, but I heard something in his voice as he shouted after me, 'See you there, then, Lucy?'

I felt something hurting deep inside me. I had thought I was a strong spinster sort of girl, happy enough to be working and living a good, healthy and quiet life; but suddenly, new thoughts were filling me. What would it be like to have a man wanting to see me every day? Perhaps to love me?

It was a shock, feeling like that. So I gathered up the empty pie dishes and baskets, hung them on Duchess's saddle, and led her away from the walls to a convenient rock where I could easily mount her. I rode home with my mind in a whirl, only calming as I reached the farm and told myself sharply to get on with the baking. It was Thursday already and there was still a lot to do.

★ ★ ★

Friday, and my two baskets were filled with all sorts of food ready for the dance. Emma had come round in the trap to collect them in the morning, and seemed friendly enough. Though she did say with a sly smile before she drove off again, 'I expect you're looking forward to dancing with Stephen, like all the other girls, aren't you? I just hope he hasn't got two left feet, like Will.' Then she flourished the whip at me and drove out of the yard.

I hadn't replied. I knew I must keep my temper where Emma was concerned; and besides, it was true, I supposed — just like all the other village girls, I had a dream of dancing with Stephen. And of keeping my distance from Alan Hannaford.

I finished the farm work early, as the afternoon slowly slid towards evening, and then spent time in my bedroom, putting on the elegant clothes that I had refreshed and ironed. As I slowly became used to the reflection in front of me looking so clean, smart and smiling, I knew I was intent on having a really good evening's outing. It would be a pleasure to leave the lonely farmhouse; and never mind dancing with Stephen or not, it would be so good to mix with my village friends, see my pies and cakes going down well, and listen to the music. Lizzie would be there too, which was really a cheering thought, for together we would laugh, tap our toes, and gossip. What else could I want?

When I reached Will's barn, music was already playing. Old Eddie Hext and his accordion were squeezing out familiar tunes. Lizzie suddenly came running up behind me, slipping her arm through mine and saying excitedly, 'You look lovely, Lucy — that skirt is so smart — and what d'you think of mine?'

I smiled at her and said truthfully, 'You've made it very well, Lizzie. And yes, I can see how it's going to spin around!'

She gave a spin just to show I was

right, and we went into the barn together, among other villagers all dressed in whatever full skirts and check shirts they could rustle up. Emma was at the door to welcome us, and I saw how her eyes widened when she looked me over.

'Goodness,' she said. 'You look quite different, Lucy!'

I had to stop my laughter, because such a doubtful compliment was typical of her. But I smiled my thanks at her. 'And you look good yourself,' I said generously, wondering how she could have afforded to buy that new dress with the full skirt and low neckline. Something Will had had to go without, I thought rather nastily. But the village knew about Emma's selfishness, and I expected many of them were thinking the same as me.

Then Will was beside us, his face full of smiles, his hair greased back and his bright check shirt as obviously new as his wife's dress was, so I forgave Emma in my mind. 'Have you set out my pies

51

and cakes, Will? I do hope there'll be enough to go round.'

He grinned. 'Don't worry, Lucy, we've only put out a few of them, keeping the rest for later on when we all get hot and hungry. Now, go and find yourself a partner and get ready for the first dance.'

As Lizzie and I went further into the barn, a voice behind me said, 'Lucy — my goodness, don't you look smart! I'll have the first dance with you. Let's go and line up, shall we?' It was Alan Hannaford, looking me all over and taking my hand in his, almost pulling me down towards the circle of hay bales and pushing me into the middle where other pairs of boys and maids were standing opposite each other. I caught Lizzie's eye and saw her grinning before she turned away to greet a handsome chap obviously asking her to partner him.

The first dance was easy, a line dance where we all followed the caller as he shouted 'Do-si-do' and we all joined in.

This was friendly and fun, we maids grinning at each other as we moved along, and allowing our partners to take our hands and sometimes pull us a bit too close to them; but it always happened at barn dances. Nothing to worry about — until the dance ended and Alan pulled me out of the dance space and into the shadowy back of the barn, where a couple of hay bales were attracting couples to go and sit out the next dance. I wanted to keep dancing, and pulled away from his hands, but he was strong; and before I knew it I had fallen onto a hay bale with him beside me, bending over me and kissing me.

I wriggled away, telling him to stop — and then, thank goodness, someone else was near me, and a deep voice said sharply, 'Come with me, Lucy. No need to rest already, surely? And you, Hannaford, keep your hands to yourself.'

I was drawn to my feet and led very firmly out of the shadows into the lamp-lit centre of the dance space, where couples were already forming up and Eddie was drinking a mug of cider before the next bit of business. I was thankful to escape from Alan; I would be sure to keep away from him for the rest of the evening. The knowledge that I was going to dance with Stephen pushed away the unpleasant thought of those unwanted kisses.

He drew me into the circle of dancers and looked at me with a big grin. 'Ready for a bit of exercise?' he asked. 'Remember your Sir Roger de Coverley, I hope? We may have to watch our feet after all these years. Hope I shan't tread on you, Lucy.'

I laughed. 'Once danced, never forgotten — I think it'll all come back to us, Stephen. Let's see how it goes, shall we?'

Eddie played a loud chord; we turned towards each other and prepared to dance as he thumped out the tune we all knew, and we curtseyed and bowed to our partners. Then the tricky part started — I held Stephen's hand tightly, hoping some of his memories would come into my bewildered mind, as we started 'lacing the boot'. We all crossed by right shoulders, going behind the next couple and so on down the set, taking hands at the bottom and then slipping back up to the top. Then 'under the bridge', and starting again from the top. But it was at the end that the real fun came — Eddie playing a thundering chord, and all of us dancing the basket figure of two couples in a ring, the men with arms joined behind the girls' backs, girls with their arms around the men's necks.

We twirled one way then the other, laughing, enjoying the fun, the music and the steps; and then our partners lifted us maids off our feet as high as they could, and we all screamed as the dance ended. Stephen looked at me and we both laughed as if we were back in the old days of growing up.

'Not bad,' he said. 'And you were as light as a feather, Lucy. It's hot in here. Think we need a sit outside — come with me, will you, maid?'

I just nodded. No need for words. Surely he knew what I was thinking — that it was better than old times; we had found each other again, and perhaps now, alone in the cool Dartmoor evening, we could speak of things that were important to us both.

I gave him my hand and he led me out into the blessed quiet and fresh air. I had no worries that watching eyes would see us and start up idle, wicked guessing as to whether we would come back into the dance or just disappear into the shadows that loomed all around the barn, promising places where we could be alone.

For a few minutes it was absolute peace. Even the music faded away for a while. A dog barked on a distant farm; a blackbird in someone's garden tuned up. Stephen, sitting beside me on a grassy bank along the village road, said, 'So how's life treating you these days, Lucy? I guess you must miss Pete a lot?'

But before I could form my reply

there were footsteps behind us, and Alan Hannaford's rough voice saying, 'Thought I'd catch you out here, Lucy; I saw you sneaking out. But you, Stephen Neal — just remember that she's my maid and she don't want to see any more of you. Got it, have you?'

Shocked, I leapt to my feet, but Stephen's big hand pulled me back and I landed on the grass again, watching as he faced up to Alan and said quietly, but with anger in his deep voice, 'Lucy Wells is no one's maid, Hannaford, and you should remember that. Understand?'

5

I ran. There was shouting behind me, and arguing voices, but suddenly a hand gripped my arm and Lizzie said, 'Where are you off to, Lucy? Don't take no notice of those silly chaps — all warmed up with ale and cider, I daresay.'

I stood quite still, sucked in a deep breath and thought how foolish it all had become, Stephen and Alan coming to blows because of me. Lizzie was staring at me, and in the cool moonlight I saw how anxious she looked. So I controlled my feelings and said quietly, 'I'm off home. Had enough of all this dancing and prancing about — I want my bed. Got to get up early tomorrow.'

I moved away, but she was there at my side. 'Good idea,' she said, her hand still on my arm. 'I'll come with you

— time for a nice quiet cup of tea, I reckon. Had enough of all that noise myself. But I'll tell you one thing, Lucy — your cakes were going like . . . well,' she guffawed, 'like hotcakes! Bet Alan'll be round first thing tomorrow wanting more.'

That brought me back to the real world; and as we reached the farmyard entrance, with Fly giving us a noisy welcome, I felt my old self again — still a bit hot after the dancing, but thinking how nice it had been to join in a village party. Though Alan's unwelcome kisses still made me frown.

'Come in then, Lizzie. If you pull the kettle over the flames, I'll find a biscuit or something and get the mugs out.'

Soon we sat close to the fire, drinking our tea and finishing the biscuits in the tin. Lizzie's eyes sparkled and she still looked wonderful in her colourful dress. 'Went well, didn't it?' she asked.

I nodded, not intending to tell her how horrid her brother had been. 'Good to see everybody getting together, and being nice and happy.'

I reminded her that Mike had been dancing with the miller's daughter from down the river, and she grinned at me and winked. 'Gossip says they're starting courting. And that's not all — even Emma seemed in a good mood. I daresay she'll organise a few neighbours to do the clearing up tomorrow! Likes to throw her weight about, does Emma. Can't imagine how Stephen puts up with her.' She stopped suddenly. 'He danced with lots of maids, I saw; and then he disappeared — with you.'

I knew she was waiting, but it took a few moments to gather my words. Then I said, slowly and with all the control I could muster, 'We went outside to get cool after that Sir Roger madness. And then . . . ' I stopped, remembering Alan's rough voice.

She finished the sentence for me. 'And then that brother of mine came to claim you.'

We looked at each other as the fire

crackled and let fall a few embers. I suddenly felt anxious. Lizzie's expression had lost its glow and pleasure. She looked worried.

I said sharply, 'Say what's on your mind, Lizzie, for I can see something's wrong.'

'Well . . . ' She pulled out the word and suddenly avoided my eyes. 'It's gossip, Lucy. You know how folks love to talk, and imagine things, and make the worst of them? Well, it's going around that you're after Stephen Neal, and there's a bet on that any day now you'll be inviting him here to Larkhill Farm.'

We stared across the dying fire's glow, and then she said, 'I think that wicked Emma started it. And you know how all the old girls with nothing to do pick these ideas up and embroider them.'

I felt a cold knot forming inside me. Yes, I knew only too well about village gossip and the wretchedness it could cause. There had been gossip about

Pete and Annie until they actually announced that they would be married after the hay harvest. And now it was about me, was it?

I lifted my head an extra inch and sat straighter in my chair, looking at Lizzie and daring her to say any more. 'Look,' I said at last, 'I don't care a tinker's cuss about what the village gossips like to say. I intend to live my life exactly as I want to — and they can make the worst of it if they choose. As it happens, I have no intention of inviting Stephen Neal to come and live here. Why should I? He can make his own arrangements; find a rented cottage or something. The only thing I'm doing for him is providing pasture for his stallion until he gets land of his own. And that's the end of it all, Lizzie. So please don't listen to any more of these horrible stories, will you? And now, let's finish the day by draining that teapot, because it's long past my bedtime, and yours too, I bet. So — here's to the end of gossip, and haven't we had a lovely evening?'

We raised our half-filled mugs and grinned at each other. I felt the bad stories fade into the background, where I hoped they would stay. Lizzie got up, twirled her skirt around, and gave me her usual big grin. 'I'm off, then,' she said, heading for the door. 'And Lucy, be sure to get on with the baking tomorrow, won't you? Otherwise you'll have Alan coming up and making a fuss. Well, goodnight, maid, and I'm glad we've had this chat. We'll always be friends, won't we, Lucy?'

I went to the door with her, looked out into the moonlight, and replied, 'Of course we will.' I added, 'Are you sure you'll be all right walking home alone?'

Her grin grew even bigger. 'We Dartmoor maids ain't afraid of a pretty green lane and a slant of moonlight, Lucy. Well, goodnight, now.' She went quickly out of the entrance and I heard her shoes tapping down the lane as I went indoors, locked the door, and went up the stairs into my bedroom.

It had been quite an exciting evening

and I found it hard to get to sleep. But the next morning had me up at the usual time, my thoughts still racing around the unpleasant news Lizzie had told me — that I was being gossiped about, and so was Stephen.

I had a quick bite of breakfast and did all the usual early-morning chores, and then the knowledge came with a flash of certainty: I must tell Stephen that the unthinking help I was offering should end. I had no wish to involve him in unpleasant chatter. He must find other pasture for Apollo as soon as the newtake wall task was completed.

I found him hard at work with Mike up on the moor and plunged straight into what I knew must be said. 'Stephen, I'm afraid I can't go on letting you graze Apollo up here. The village is talking about us.'

He put down his stone hammer, turned and stared at me. 'Talking about us? What, you and me? What on earth about?'

I swallowed the lump forming in my

tight throat. 'Someone thinks we might be planning to marry or — something — because you're using my land.'

The blue eyes, instead of reflecting the beautiful sky above him, turned icy, and I felt a cold chill run through my body. Stephen, angry, could be a different man. I began to stutter stupidly. 'It's just gossip, of course. No reason for anyone to think . . . I mean — well, how silly, isn't it? You and I, of all people!'

He just stood there, looking at me. I knew I was flustered, and no doubt looked it. But still, I had to make him understand. My voice was low and hesitant as I said, 'I think someone started talking about us because of last night, when we left the barn together. Someone's said a few nasty words, and they've caught on.' Still he said nothing. I felt a fool and added, 'Perhaps it was Alan, because you pushed him away from me.'

At last he spoke, his voice deep and intense. 'Or someone else with a wicked mind.'

I knew at once that he meant Emma Neal. After all, she had been saying things that could easily have started rumours throughout the village. But I shook my head. I didn't want any more trouble between Stephen and his brother.

'Can't think who, Stephen,' I lied. 'But it doesn't matter, does it? The main thing is that you must take Apollo and go somewhere else.'

'Away from you, and Larkhill Farm.'

I sighed. It was so horrible, and so obvious, that it was Emma's mischief which had led us into this difficult situation. But I knew he was right. 'Yes,' I said very quietly. 'Away from Larkhill.'

'And away from you, Lucy?'

It was a question which I found hard to answer, so I simply nodded and said a barely audible, 'Yes, Stephen.'

I wanted to stand there forever, his eyes looking so keenly into mine. My body was suddenly vibrant with new thoughts; Stephen had come to mean more to me than just an old childhood friend. But I couldn't let him know. For his own good, he needed to accept what I was trying to show — that I was a strong girl who had no ideas of marriage, and simply wanted him to leave me and my farm alone. To go somewhere else. Because he had to go — and not just from me, but from Emma and Will, who seemed to be determined to make life difficult for him. I wanted him and Apollo to find a distant farm where he could work at making his dream of a stud come true. So I told myself this moment had to stop.

I took a step away from him, turned towards Duchess harnessed nearby, and said over my shoulder, 'I'm very grateful for the work you've done with Mike. He could never have finished the job by himself, and I shall hope to hear news of you settling down on your own farm in the near future. So I'll say goodbye, Stephen.'

I allowed myself a last glance at him, then wished I hadn't. The cold blue eyes had thawed and were looking at me in a way I had never seen before. Almost as if I had said something ridiculous that he couldn't believe. But he said nothing. After a pause, he simply bowed his head and turned back to the last broken wall, on which Mike was still working.

I had expected at least a friendly farewell, perhaps even thanks for allowing Apollo to enjoy my pasture for the last few days — not this out-of-hand dismissal. Yet, as I mounted Duchess, it struck me that perhaps this was the best thing to happen. Stephen would get out of my life and I would be left to get on with what I had always expected my future to be: lonely years of hard, unrelenting work.

I rode home, thankful for the wind that dried the tears rolling down my cheeks, and also with a new sense of reality filling me. I must simply accept life as it happened; and what had just happened was that my newtake walls were repaired, and I had lost someone who I hoped might still be my friend.

But at the same time I knew I had made the right decision. And life goes on, doesn't it?

But what went on as I rode into Larkhill's yard was that Alan Hannaford came to meet me, his face set in hard lines, saying with a chill in his voice, 'Been up to spend time with that Stephen, have you? Well, Lucy, I can tell you the village is getting excited, you know — asking when the wedding will be. But I shan't be there, maid, not when I thought you and I had an understanding.'

He glowered at me before going on. 'I'm wondering how you can possibly do this to me. After all, we're friends, and I'm selling your tarts and pies and things — you could at least show a bit of gratitude, I think. So how about asking me in for a chat? I think we have a lot to talk about.' His voice deepened and his eyes narrowed. 'That is, if you still want me to sell your cakes.'

I felt numb, mostly with disappointment and dismay at losing Stephen's friendship. But now I experienced an extra chill, because I realised that Alan was going to try and blackmail me into marrying him.

6

We went into the kitchen and I noticed that Fly followed us in, which was unusual. He generally stayed out in the yard, watching everything happening, and happy enough in his kennel. But this morning he came up to the fire and sat there looking up at me as if he wanted something.

I hung up my coat and hat and invited Alan to pull a stool up to the fire, though I wasn't at all pleased at having him there; there was too much to do. But he wanted to talk, so I pulled the kettle closer over the fire and collected the milk from the dairy.

'So,' I said at last, watching as he looked all around the room, seeming to take note of everything, 'what's this all about, Alan? And please could we make it short, as there's all the baking to do.'

'That's what it's about, Lucy — your

baking, and my shop selling the cakes and things. I think you know quite well what's in my mind.' He was smiling, a sort of self-satisfied smile that I didn't like.

I went to the dresser and fetched two mugs, saying as I returned to the table and the fire, 'Yes, I do know. You're trying to force me to say I'll agree to marry you — that is, if I want to continue making my pies and cakes and things to sell.' I fixed him with a steely stare. 'Well, Alan, I definitely won't agree to anything as underhand as that. Goodness, it's a sort of blackmail, isn't it? But if you won't sell my wares, then I'll take them somewhere else to be sold.'

He grinned, which was something I wasn't prepared for. 'Don't think you will, Lucy. Not with the way the village feels about you and Stephen at the moment. You're heading to be a scarlet woman, you know, the way you're going on.' His grin grew broader and more unpleasant.

I jumped to my feet, almost upsetting

the milk jug as I did so. 'I've never heard such nonsense!' I cried. 'Scarlet woman indeed — simply because I asked Stephen Neal to do a bit of work for me?'

'And went out and sat in the darkness with him last night,' he reminded me.

'What if I did? At least he wasn't trying to kiss me, as you were — or have you decided to forget that nasty little scene?'

By now I was really angry, my voice loud. I glared down at him. 'I think you'd better go, Alan, and never mind about the pies and cakes. I shan't be bringing you any more — so just get out and don't come bothering me again.'

I stepped away from the table and watched him slowly get up, grin never fading, and then very slowly walk towards me. There was a yelp; he looked down and swore.

'Damn dog! What's it doing in here? Why don't you keep it outside like every other farmer does?' He half-bent down and lifted his arm as if to strike Fly, but I reached out in time and pulled him away.

'Don't you dare touch my dog! Just go, Alan, I tell you. Go!'

I strode to the door, flung it open and waited there until he came up to me, eyes burning and voice harsh. He half-whispered, passing me, 'You'll be sorry about all this, Lucy. Just wait and see.' Then he marched out through the doorway and into the yard.

I waited there until he was safely in the road heading for the village, and then I went inside and shut the door behind me with a bang, suddenly feeling rather upset. Fly was lying on his side, panting and looking at me with wild eyes as he fought to get his breath.

I went down on my knees, hand on his head which felt unnaturally hot, and ran the other hand over his body. He yelped again, but this time I realised that, although Alan hadn't hurt him, poor old Fly was very ill. I knelt there, wondering what on earth I could do to help him. The only vet was in Widecombe, a good few miles away; and I thought no vet, however clever, could help an old dog who was probably ending his days. I remembered the time, so long ago, when Fly had come home in Pa's pocket, a birthday present from market for me. How long? I didn't like to think.

I reached up and found a rug hanging on the back of the fireside chair and covered him with it. He raised his head and looked at me, then closed his eyes and once again rested his head on the floor.

I stayed there until I saw the dear old dog had gone. I left him there in the warm while I once again rode Duchess up to the moor and told Mike he must come home and help me find a quiet place where we could lay Fly in his final sleep.

I didn't think about Stephen, but he must have heard what I told Mike, for he came up to me and put his hand around my shoulder. 'Better to die like that, Lucy, than linger on in pain,' he said, and I heard the note of warm sympathy in his deep voice. It helped me somehow; and as Mike and I returned to the farmhouse, I felt stronger and better able to face up to the inevitable sadness of life and death.

We took the old dog, wrapped in the rug, out into the meadow; and after Mike had dug a hole near the hedge where he had so loved to sniff out rabbits, we placed him there. Then we went back to the farm and I took out what was left of a small bottle of cider, forcing myself to smile at Mike, who looked as wretched as I felt. I said, 'A sip of this to speed Fly on his way, eh, Mike?'

So we drank a last toast, and then suddenly life was all about us again.

Mike said, 'I'll get back to the wall, missus. Job's nearly done; us'll finish it later today.' He went to the door, stopped and looked at me over his shoulder. 'Or do you want me to stay around this afternoon?'

The kindness of his thought and the

warmth of the expression on his young face brought me new strength. I was able to smile back properly and say, 'No, Mike, I'm all right. But thanks for offering.'

I saw relief in his smile as he opened the door, saying, 'S'pose you'll have to think about gettin' a new dog, then, won't you, missus? Can't work the sheep proper without one.'

When he had gone and I was alone in the kitchen, measuring out sugar and butter, and going to fetch eggs from the dairy, I thought about that last remark. Yes, Fly would have to be replaced — but not yet. First I would have to get used to the fact that my old friend was no longer around.

As I mixed cakes and made pastry, my thoughts returned to all that Alan Hannaford had said to me. I felt myself growing ever more determined to stop all the wicked gossip, and instead encourage the villagers to buy all my wares and turn my apparently bad reputation into one of achievement and helpfulness in our small community.

I got through that day without too many sad thoughts because, of course, there were all the usual tasks to be completed. By the time I went to bed I was tired out, but pleased with myself. I was proving, if only to myself, that I was a strong woman who could live life as she wanted to.

No doubt Alan Hannaford had other thoughts; I knew Emma Neal did, and perhaps Stephen also wondered a bit. But I was pleased with myself, and when I woke next morning I at once thought of how I could make myself a bit stronger.

If I could no longer sell my goods in the village, then I would start a stall right here at Larkhill, and persuade the villagers to take a short walk up the hill to collect their pies and cakes and tarts. I could see it in my mind's eye — a nicely painted board nailed to the gatepost in the lane: HOMEMADE CAKES, TARTS AND PIES, ALL MADE ON THE PREMISES BY LUCY IN

THE LARKHILL KITCHEN. PLEASE COME IN.

I tried the idea out on Mike while we snatched our breakfast, and watched his expression as for a long moment he sat there and thought, halfway through his bowl of porridge and honey. Finally he looked at me and frowned . . . but the frown turned into a grin as he said, 'Think of all those boots coming over your doorstep, missus — cos everybody will want to come and see what you're up to in the kitchen, let alone buy one of yourn nice buns or sommat.'

I spooned out another helping of porridge to encourage him and said, 'Do you really think people will come, Mike? Be honest with me, please.'

He nodded and said, 'I do. But what about the farm work, missus? Can't do that and bake cakes, can 'ee?'

I said rather sharply, 'Well, I've been doing just that for several months, Mike. Why should I stop now?'

'Cos old Joe ain't comin' back, is he, and I reckon you need some help if you'm to do two jobs much longer.'

His breakfast finished, he took the empty bowl and his mug to the sink, then pulled on his jacket. 'Gotta go, now, missus, but I'm sure glad we finished those ol' walls. Where's Stephen Neal got to, I wonder? Looking for somewhere to live, he said afore he went off last night.'

I stood up a bit straighter and didn't meet his curious eyes. 'I can't help you there, I'm afraid. Mike, if you think my idea is a good one, please will you make the board I shall need? And then I can paint it — I think a nice white background with big black letters, don't you? Everyone will see that. Could you do it tonight, please?'

He just nodded, stamped towards the door, and disappeared. I heard him laughing as he went towards the stable to harness Duchess. In my turn, I went outside and spent the next ten minutes or so milking Daisy, quietly murmuring my new plan to her. But she made no comment.

That evening, the daily work finished, the fire crackling nicely and a good meal inside us, Mike and I were sitting by the hearth. I watched him working on a big square of old wood he'd found in an outshed, carefully fashioning it into the notice board I could see in my imagination.

Before we went up to bed that evening the board was resting on the kitchen table. Tomorrow, when I found the time, I would very carefully paint my words over it.

The next morning I grinned at Mike as he put on his cap and jacket and prepared for the day's first chores, and said happily, 'By the time you come home for dinner, it'll be up out there on the gate post. And with any luck, the first customers will come during the afternoon. So I'm going to make extra jam tarts and biscuits — after all, I'll have to offer them refreshments, won't I?'

He paused at the pighouse wall,

where old Ebenezer was snuffling away on the inside, asking for his breakfast. He looked at me seriously. 'Come on, missus, you can't afford to give away your good things — I don't have much schoolin', but I do know that if you run a business you have to make a profit, an' you won't make much if you gives it all away.' I smiled as I watched him pick up the swill bucket and go into Ebenezer's little house.

As I returned to my duties, I realised Mike had been right the previous day — my new business would take up more time than I really had to spare. I needed some help. I quickly ran through the names of all the villagers, and I stopped when I came to Lizzie Hannaford. Could I persuade dear Lizzie to come and be my new assistant? But even as I thought it, I knew Alan wouldn't be happy if she did.

I got out the paintpot and a clean brush and began planning out my big capital letters. But it was a slow job, and when Mike came home for dinner I had nothing prepared — just a bright new notice board and yesterday's half-eaten mutton pie, and a couple of baked potatoes I'd had the sense to put in the ashes after breakfast. That was when I knew for a fact I couldn't go on this way. I definitely needed help from somewhere.

7

Next morning Eli the postman knocked on the door while I was washing the breakfast dishes. Once these were finished, I intended to do the necessary outside chores and then come in again and have a really good bake.

'Mornin' Lucy,' he said, handing me a dull-looking buff envelope. 'What's this with puddings and cakes, then? Alan down at the shop says he won't take no more of them — why's that?' His mischievous eyes twinkled beneath his peaked cap. 'Had a lover's fight, have 'ee?'

I thought crossly, *All that old gossip again*, but out loud I said, 'No, Eli, just a new arrangement. And Alan's not my lover to be having a fight with, so I'd be grateful if on your round you'd let everyone know that.'

Suddenly I remembered a few biscuits left in the half-empty tin. I took them out, wrapped them in a scrap of paper, and handed the little packet to him, saying with a smile, 'Here's a tasty bite to cheer you on your way, Eli.'

'Thank 'ee.' He pocketed it with a big grin. 'Well, gotta be off — but I'll spread your news, Lucy. Cakes and pies, eh?' He frowned for a moment and then the grin returned, bigger than ever. 'My li'l maid's birthday is next Friday, so I'll tell my missus to come and buy a cake before that.'

I really did smile then. 'Yes, I could make a special cake, Eli, with icing on the top. Will that do?'

He paused in the open doorway. 'Sounds good. I'll tell 'er as we've put in an order, and she can bring the li'l maid up to collect it during the week. Say, Thursday — all right, Lucy?'

Out in the yard he stopped, turned and added, 'Lost ol' Fly, have 'ee? Well, I'll keep me eyes open for a new dog, shall I?'

'Thank you, Eli, if you would.' My

smile suddenly died as I missed Fly all over again.

Another wave, another grin, and Eli mounted his bicycle and set off on his next round.

With Daisy milked, the hens fed and the water pail in the dairy refilled from the well, I returned to the kitchen table and set about making a fruitcake and a treacle tart, and refilling the biscuit tin with shortbread. Then I made a pie for dinner.

After that, sitting in the cane chair thinking how well I had done, I found a bit of clean paper and wrote: ELI, POSTMAN, ONE BIRTHDAY CAKE, READY THURSDAY, 27TH AUGUST.

My first order! I was pleased and proud, for surely this was the beginning of my new little business.

I was clearing things away when footsteps sounded in the yard and Lizzie peered around the open door. 'Goodness, it's so exciting Lucy, you setting up here — and I can tell you Alan's hopping mad! What fun — and, oh, can I please be part of it?'

Dear Lizzie. She came dancing into the room and gave me a hug.

'Here's a kiss for luck! And I'm sure you'll sell and sell — your cakes are so lovely!'

I hugged her back, grateful for her warm friendship and all that cheering enthusiasm — and, of course, the wonderful offer of help. 'Come and sit down,' I said. 'I'll make a pot of tea and we'll have a bit of shortbread to celebrate!' I was glad to have an excuse to rest, and I wanted to talk seriously to her about helping. We sat opposite each other beside the crackling fire, and Lizzie — being Lizzie — let all the local gossip flow out.

'Yes, Alan's in a real bother, and is trying hard to find someone else to sell him cakes, but we all know you're the best cook in the village. I expect he'll have to go to the bakery in Moreton, and that'll make him even madder!'

'Well — ' I started, but she was off again.

'And Emma Neal's telling everyone

that her baby will win the most beautiful baby competition at Widecombe Fair in September. Will tells her to stop crowing cos it's not born yet, but once Emma starts no one can stop her!'

I asked, 'And when it is due, Lizzie?' 'Quite soon, I think — let's hope she'll quieten down when she's got a screaming li'l maid or boy to look after.'

As I poured mugs of tea and Lizzie munched her shortbread, I thought of Stephen staying at the farm in all that noise and rowdiness, and tried to arrange the words I wanted to say, but was finding it hard to do so. Then Lizzie said them for me.

'Have you any news of Stephen Neal, Lucy? Even Will doesn't know where's he's gone, although his stallion is still at the farm. And that makes Will angry.'

I took a deep breath. 'Why ask me, Lizzie? I've no idea where he might be — just looking for some land and a place to live, I expect.'

I turned away because she was

staring at me as if surprised, and I thought bitterly how busily village gossip must have spread about us. As I refilled the teapot I said crossly, 'You can forget all that silly talk about us, Lizzie — there's absolutely nothing between Stephen and me.'

'Oh,' was all she said, her expression of disbelief adding the unsaid words. So quickly I changed the subject.

'Lizzie,' I began, meeting her curious gaze, 'I do need help with this new little business — and you've offered, so I wonder . . . could you possibly spare me an hour every morning? I mean, you could do the selling and packing up when customers come while I deal with the chores in the yard.' I added, 'And of course I would pay you.'

'Hmmm,' she mused, pushing over her mug for a refill, and then grinning at me. 'Of course I could — I'd love to help. But it seems to me that what you really need is a man to help with the farmwork, isn't it? And then you'd be free to entertain your customers in the kitchen and take more orders.'

I saw mischief in her bright green eyes, and sighed. 'Oh Lizzie, just say you'll come for an hour every day — and let's forget about having a man here at Larkhill, please. I really don't want one!'

We laughed together. Then as footsteps sounded, we both turned towards the door — and there was Stephen Neal, looking at us and smiling.

'Can I come in?' he asked, and I was so surprised that all I could do was nod my head.

'Of course,' I said quickly, adding, because I couldn't think of anything else to say, 'I think there's a cup left in the pot.'

I turned away from his searching gaze, fussing about finding another mug and more milk from the dairy. When I returned, I found he had pulled a stool from under the table, and now we were three people sitting comfortably by the fire.

Lizzie giggled; I guessed she had seen

my flushed cheeks. But I was glad she was there, her chatter keeping Stephen looking her way and no longer at me. When the chatter finished, however, he was looking at me again.

'So your business is underway, Lucy? I thought the noticeboard was very eye-catching. Any customers yet?'

That gave me a chance to start talking about my plans, which stopped me feeling embarrassed at the way he was looking at me. 'Yes; I have one customer already, ordering a birthday cake. I'm waiting for all the others to come and see what's going on here at Larkhill — because of course all the old gossips will want to know, won't they?'

Lizzie cut in, a chuckle in her voice. 'And take their minds off what they're saying about you and Stephen, perhaps.'

Stephen's voice was suddenly sharp, and I saw an icy glint in his blue eyes as he turned to look at her. 'That bad, is it, Lizzie? Exactly what've you heard, then?'

She had the grace to blush, but was chuckling as she said, 'That Lucy wants to marry you! Why, it's the talk of the village. But I know Lucy has other ideas — only just now she said she doesn't want a man at Larkhill.'

Stephen turned to look at me, and there was a new glint in his eyes which I thought was amusement. My temper rose. How dare he laugh at me, just because I had strong ideas about my own capabilities?

Rapidly I got to my feet, saying shortly, 'Well, I haven't the time to sit here and gossip, even if you two have.' I whisked the empty mugs off the table and took them to the sink, saying over my shoulder, 'Lizzie, I shall expect you for an hour tomorrow morning. Please do come. And Stephen,' I added, turning and fixing him with my angry gaze, 'you'd be better off looking for that cottage and land you so badly want, instead of just sitting here and wasting my time.'

There was a moment's awkward

silence. Lizzie shrugged her shoulders, then grinned at me as she headed for the door. 'All right, Lucy,' she said. 'I just hope that temper of yours won't frighten all your customers away.' Then she disappeared across the yard.

I tightened my mouth and made a big business of looking into the oven to see if the pie was done. Stephen rose, pushed the stool back under the table and said, 'I get the message — no man here at Larkhill. But I'm afraid you may have to change your mind, Lucy.'

His voice was quiet, but I recognised the warning note. Turning, I saw wicked amusement in his eyes, and felt uncomfortably anxious. What was he talking about? I said nothing, but simply stared at him.

He came and took me by the hand, leading me to the open door. I was so startled at his touch that I went obediently. His hand was strong and hard, but so warm and full of energy that I suddenly enjoyed the feeling.

Out in the yard he took me to the

sycamore tree beneath which Will Neal's pony trap waited. The back was piled with groceries, and in the middle was an old basket, fastened with a worn leather strap. I stared at it — it seemed to be moving; then I heard something scraping inside it. A short, sharp bark made me open my eyes wider and lean over the side of the trap.

'What on earth — ?' I asked, but some instinct told me what to expect, and I felt all my old annoyance dying away.

Stephen said, in his usual quiet voice, 'I've just made my peace with Emma by doing her shopping for her. In Moreton Market I found someone who needs a new home — and I thought it would be a new companion for you, Lucy. Here, look inside.'

He undid the strap and held the basket top open. At once a small black and white dog leaped up, eyes fixed on me, and a wet nose pushed itself at my hand. I looked at the collie puppy sitting there and felt my anger with Stephen Neal dying; indeed, I felt tears welling behind

my eyelids as I realised, with an unexpected tingle of pleasure, that he had
gone to the trouble of finding me this
replacement for Fly. Then a new thought
swept through my mind — Stephen was
a kind man, and I would do well to try
and help him with his problems.

I stroked the rough fur of the pup,
who was now trying to leap out of the
basket, and turned to Stephen standing
beside me. He was looking at me with
warmth in those blue eyes. 'I don't know
what to say,' I muttered as the puppy
pawed at my arms and demanded to be
picked up and cuddled.

'What I'd like to hear is that you're
pleased,' said Stephen, and I felt his
smile envelop me as I struggled with
the restless animal in my arms. I started
to laugh, and the pup wriggled enough
to stand up and lick my face.

'I am! Oh Stephen, I'm so pleased,
and it's so kind and thoughtful of you
to have found him. What shall we call
him?'

Stephen frowned and put out his

hand to stroke the dog, which at once nipped at his fingers. 'I think he was meant to be called Nip, and perhaps that's as good as any name — but you must choose.'

I sucked in a huge breath and felt delight spreading through me. 'I don't know. Yes, I suppose Nip would be all right.'

'Or what about Boy? After all, he's the new man about Larkhill, and he deserves to have a title, don't you think?'

I saw the laughter in his eyes and knew he was taunting me once again, but at this particular moment I had no reason to be angry with him. I was so grateful, and was even beginning to think that he wasn't the patronising and annoying man who had lived in my mind over the past few weeks. I saw his point, and was ready to acknowledge it. Dropping a kiss on the puppy's head, I said meekly, 'Yes. Thank you. Boy is a perfect name. And now I'd better take him indoors and show him his new home.'

I turned towards the house, trying to restrain the newly christened Boy from leaping out of my arms. Stephen's voice followed me. 'And I must get back to Emma and just hope I've got everything her ladyship ordered. Good luck with the cakes, Lucy, and I'll see you sometime.'

He drove the trap out of the yard while I went into the kitchen. As I set down the new man around the house, I suddenly realised I was no longer on my own — and it was thanks to Stephen, who had bothered, among his own problems, to think about mine.

8

I had an unexpected visitor next morning. I was returning to the kitchen, having loaded Lizzie's basket with all the things I had cooked yesterday. She was sitting on a little camp stool beside the yard wall, waiting for customers, and I heard her laughing and talking to someone. At once I thought of Stephen, who had been in my mind ever since Boy had arrived the previous day. But it was Will, his brother, who finally knocked at the open door and called, 'Lucy — can I come in?'

'Of course, Will. Nice to see you — you don't come this way very often. Come and sit down.'

He lowered himself into the cane chair, which made it creak even more than usual. Then he looked around the kitchen, and up at me as I stood by the table. His tanned face split into an attractive smile. 'So here you are, Lucy, among all your cookery things. I suppose you know the village is full of the news of you selling cakes and tarts up here at Larkhill, instead of at Alan's shop?'

'Yes,' I said carefully, not wanting to hear any more about the row I was supposed to have had with Alan. 'Just a new idea — and with Lizzie helping me, it seems a good one.' I grinned and began remembering all the arguments Will and I had had when we were children. It was nice to have him here now without any bother, I thought, amused.

'So what brings you up to Larkhill, Will? A good big order for some of my treacle tarts, perhaps?'

He chuckled. 'Cor, they were good, those we had on our picnics. I wouldn't mind having one again anytime. But things are different now, you see.' The laughter died and he looked serious. 'The thing is, Lucy, Emma's got it into her head that she wants to make a really good cake to celebrate the birth of our child, which isn't far off now. Next week sometime, it should be.' He fidgeted in the chair and put out a hand to stroke Boy, who tried to jump into his lap, and then his expression changed. 'And so she wondered if you'd be kind enough to let her see a book of recipes so that she can choose one and know it'll turn out well. She's not a great cook, as you know ... but, I mean, all your cakes are successes, aren't they?'

I nodded. 'Well, pretty good, on the whole.'

'That's what she said.' His smile returned. 'So would you lend her your book for a few days, Lucy? She's so keen to get the cake made before she has the baby that there probably isn't too much time to spare.'

What was this? Emma wanted to make cakes and be friends? That could only be good news. Of course she could borrow my mother's old book. 'Yes,

Will, she can have it for a few days. It's full of good old recipes — my mother was a wonderful cook — and I'm only too glad to get Emma started on becoming a cook herself. Wait a moment and I'll get it for you.'

I went to the cupboard where the ancient exercise book with a soft, rather worn-out dark blue cover lay, carefully stowed away from butter and eggs and messy ingredients that might make it even weaker. I found some paper and wrapped it up before handing it over to Will, who took it and stored it away in his vast pocket.

'Good of you, Lucy,' he said, getting up and looking at me with a friendly grin. 'Don't worry, she'll look after it — a proper bit of memory for you, that book, I'd say.'

'Yes, Will. Full of thoughts of my mother.'

I nodded at him, and then was surprised to hear him say rather diffidently, 'Er . . . about Stephen, Lucy. I hear as he's been helping you and Mike with the old newtake walls and grazing Apollo on your pasture land. Good of you to take him on.' Turning, he fixed me with his deep brown eyes and I saw how his expression had changed; gone was friendliness, and in its place I thought I read some sort of pleading.

At once I stood a little straighter. 'That's right, Will. But we heard the village gossip, so I asked Stephen to take the stallion and leave the farm. We don't want that sort of talk, do we?'

Staring at me, he simply nodded, and we looked at each other for a long moment before I made myself ask the question running around my mind lately. 'What is Stephen doing about finding a new home? Because, of course, you won't want him at Hayes Farm once the baby comes, will you? Too much for Emma to do.'

I'd hardly finished my questions when he broke in. 'Too many rows as well. Those two just don't get along. Be best for him to set up his own home, and I told him so. Which is why he's disappeared lately — been out looking for land and a tenant farm, I suppose. But now he's back, and still no new home.' He paused, and then looked at me very keenly. 'So he needs someone friendly enough to offer him a room where he can settle till he finds what he wants.' His eyes had become slightly magnetic, and I couldn't stop looking at them as I realised what he was getting at.

Faintly, I said, 'And you think, because I helped him once, I might do so again? Have him here at Larkhill until he gets settled in his own place?' My voice had risen higher, and I saw how suddenly anxious Will looked. Then he revealed the master plan he had been concocting.

'But Emma said that she thought you were after Stephen — wanted to marry him — so coming here wouldn't be . . . Well, nothing for the gossips, not if you were married.'

Speechless, I stared at him. He

couldn't be saying such a thing! I pulled Boy towards me and held him tightly, my hands trembling in his black fur while my mind somersaulted, trying to come to terms with what Will had suggested.

He was silent, waiting for my answer. As Boy wriggled free of my grasp, I knew I must be sensible and find the right words to make a logical reply. They came slowly, but I heard my voice sounding steady, and felt confidence returning. I looked into his eyes without any more confusion or embarrassment.

'Emma, and the rest of the village, have got it all wrong, Will. Of course I've always been fond of Stephen — and you — because we shared our childhoods, but I have no wish to marry him.' I paused, remembering happy days, before going on. 'In fact, I shall never marry. It's a decision I came to quite recently. You see, I'm content to stay here and keep the family farm running. So, no — I'm not going to offer Stephen a room, although I expect he would be grateful if I did.' I paused again, wondering how frank I could be, before deciding to continue. 'I don't think he enjoys being at Hayes Farm with Emma and you, Will.' I stopped then, wondering if he would take exception to those last words, but I felt honesty between us was important, and I was relieved when slowly he nodded.

'You're right, Lucy. Stephen and I have always argued — even fought, and now Emma's finding it hard to have us both there, especially with the baby coming so soon.' Now it was his turn to pause, looking at me to see if I understood the situation. 'So you see, it's important that he moves out pretty quickly. And that's why I'd hoped . . . ' Breaking off, he grinned a bit, but it was not the happy smile I was used to. He added, 'Well, there it is; and if that's how you feel, then I respect that, Lucy.'

We smiled at each other. Will got up and put on his hat. He gave Boy, now dancing around his feet, a pat on the head and walked towards the door.

Sudden guilt overtook me then. Will was such an old friend, I couldn't let him go without making amends for not being more helpful. 'Wait a minute, Will — I want to give you something.' Hurriedly I found a newly baked treacle tart, put it a paper bag, and took it to him.

He stopped at the door, looked inside the bag, and smiled. At last he gave me one of those easy, big smiles that I remembered from games and picnics on the moor so many years ago. 'A treacle tart! Thanks, Lucy; that brings back a few memories of happier days.' He hesitated, then bent towards me and kissed my cheek. 'You're a good maid, Lucy,' he said quietly, then went into the yard where his pony waited. I stood in the doorway and watched him mount, wave and ride out of yard, having a laugh with Lizzie as he did so.

'I've got my treacle tart in my pocket, Lizzie, so I shan't be buying any of your goods today,' he called back over his shoulder as he left.

I called Boy, who was noisily chasing one of the hens, and together we went back into the kitchen, where he settled on the rug I'd put beside the fire. I sat down in the empty cane chair and thought. And in my thoughts, Stephen stood looking at me, his eyes warm and friendly. The guilt came back, overwhelming me. Had I given Will the wrong answer? Did I really intend to remain an old maid for the rest of my life?

Eventually I came to my senses, got up and began doing all the chores that so far had remained undone this morning. Thank goodness Mike had milked Daisy and separated the milk before setting out for the higher moorland to see to the cattle, leaving me to deal with the other daily duties. So now, a bit later than usual, I fed the hens and gave a bucket of swill to Ebenezer the pig, then looked into the granary and its sacks of feed and flour and meal. They were all right for the moment, but they would soon need restocking, I thought — and I firmly told myself I mustn't let my new baking business make me neglect the farm. After all, I'd told Will I was content to be at Larkhill and would stay here, so I must make sure everything was going on all right.

Lizzie called out as she came into the yard beside me carrying her basket, which I saw with delight was nearly empty. 'Lucy, I've had a good morning — lots of people coming and buying your goodies. Some of them would have liked to come in to see you, but I said you were too busy as I knew Will was with you.'

'You've done very well, Lizzie. Come in now and have a sit-down by the fire.'

I saw from her expression that she longed to know what Will and I had been talking about, but I wasn't going to tell her. I loved Lizzie and she was a wonderful friend, but she was a proper gossip, too. So we went indoors and had a mug of tea and a piece of shortbread left over from her sales basket.

'Who came and bought?' I asked curiously, and she laughed.

'Surely you can guess! The old ladies who don't have enough to do — Mrs. Hext, Miss Stanley . . . even the vicar's wife, Mrs. Greening, though she's always busy; I guess she was just curious like the others. She said she thought there would be a big christening party at the Manor quite soon, and she would suggest your cakes and tarts, Lucy. I tell you, you're in everyone's mind at the moment!'

Yes, I thought, *but not exactly how I would like to be*. But I laughed with her and gave her an apple pie and a bowl of cream to take home along with her wages, for helping me so willingly.

The day went on, and after dinner I took Boy out on a leash to look at the sheep on the hill. At first he didn't know what to make of them, especially when the old ram advanced on him with lowered horns, but soon his fright disappeared and I felt from his pulling on the leash that he was keen to run free. Then I realised, with special thanks to Stephen for giving him to me, that he had the makings of a good sheep dog. Not as experienced, of course, as dear old Fly, but he would improve all the time.

By the time I had inspected a few limping legs and put on the soft soap from my pocket, the sheep began grazing again, and I knew I must go home and start the everlasting baking. There must be enough goodies, as Lizzie called them, to fill her basket tomorrow morning.

As we turned around and slowly walked home I watched the setting sun painting the sky with a palette of unearthly and beautiful colours, and felt my love for Dartmoor and Larkhill Farm filling me, telling me I must always stay here, come what may. I went indoors feeling a lot happier than I had been all day, and set about my baking with a clear, bright mind.

9

Baking, baking — it filled my mind and took up far too much time, so that the daily chores, both in the yard and up on the moorland, caring for cattle and sheep, were somehow squeezed into the day and rushed past before I knew what was happening. Mike, of course, was as helpful as he could be, and I saw him looking at me with a worried expression. I felt myself becoming more and more tired, but there was no way I could alter things. My cakes, tarts, biscuits and pies were selling very fast, with people seeming to enjoy traipsing up to Larkhill to buy them. Some took notice of what I'd written on the board and came tapping at the kitchen door.

Of course I welcomed them, offered them tea if the kettle was on the boil, and listened to what they thought of my wares. Mostly it was complimentary, though Miss Stanley didn't much like the apple pie she had bought during the week, making another journey to let me know that in her young days cooks didn't use spices to make dishes more attractive — oh no, they just let the apples speak for themselves. Privately I thought a few cloves, and even a spoonful of cinnamon, made a wonderful taste in a pie; but I didn't say so.

Lizzie, as ever, was my great helper, arriving every morning with her big smile and some sort of news to make me laugh as we packed the goodies into the basket. But one morning her news didn't even make me smile.

'Stephen's had a big row with Emma, who's turned him out of the house. She's more difficult now, expecting the baby any day — so of course he didn't argue, but just left.'

I thought for a moment. 'And Apollo? Where's the stallion gone? Not left at Hayes Farm, surely?'

Lizzie piled some paper bags together, then stared at me. 'No. He's taken Apollo.'

Something in her expression worried me. 'But where've they gone? Has he found a new home yet? Will Apollo have somewhere to graze?' I felt worry invading me. Stephen, on the moor somewhere? If he had found a tenant farm with a bit of land, then wonderful, and I could stop thinking about him. But if not . . . I looked into Lizzie's anxious eyes. 'You know where he is; so go on, tell me,' I entreated her.

'No need to be so worried, Lucy. You know Stephen; he'll always find his way around things. I expect he's going around the agents in Moreton and Tavistock even now, looking for his farm with its land.'

'Tavistock.' Pete and Annie lived there. My mind circled a few times, and I wondered if Pete could help Stephen in any way. Could I get over there and ask Pete if he would take on Apollo until Stephen was fixed up with his own land? But it would take most of my day if I did. And then I saw Lizzie staring at me, and realised I had many other things in my life that needed thought and activity, so I must just forget Stephen.

I repeated that silently in my mind as I left Lizzie with her basket of goodies. She was already chatting to old Herbie Moss, who had come stomping up the hill and saying his missus wanted to see if my mutton pies were as good as hers. I went back into the kitchen and carried on baking. And then I remembered that Eli would be calling for the birthday cake tomorrow morning, so I got out the icing sugar and the silver balls and got on with the decorations, and tried to stop thinking about anything else. As if to help me, Boy came and lay down on his rug beside me in front of the fire. I was suddenly able to smile again, and tell myself how good life was.

When Lizzie came in an hour later with an empty basket, I made us a good hot cup of tea and cut into a sponge cake that I had been going to keep for tomorrow's sales. Suddenly it seemed far more important to share it with Lizzie.

'You know,' began Lizzie, halfway through a mouthful, 'what you really need is to set up your own shop. I mean, so many people enjoy your baking that I'm sure you would do well.' She giggled. 'And wouldn't that be a shock to brother Alan!'

I frowned, staring at her. 'I couldn't possibly do that, Lizzie. I have the farm to run, with only Mike to help, and all the baking as well! Goodness, having to be in a shop all day . . . well, that would never give me time for the farm.'

'Hmm.' She paused and then said, 'I could help run the shop. Would that make it possible?'

'Certainly not,' I said firmly. 'Even though you give up an hour every morning, you still have to work with your family, don't you?'

She pulled a face. 'Well, I suppose you're right. But if you got more help with the farm, then a shop would be possible.'

I saw the way her mind was running, so got up, saying briskly, 'A good idea,

Lizzie, and thank you, but I'm not doing it. And now I must finish decorating Eli's birthday cake — he's calling for it tomorrow.'

She nodded, got up and went towards the door, before turning and looking back at me. 'See you tomorrow then, Lucy — and if I hear any more news of Stephen, I'll let you know.' Our eyes met and she added quietly, 'I know you're worried about him.'

Before I could answer she was gone, and I was left with a small voice in my head whispering, *She's right, isn't she?*

* * *

Boy and I were having a half-hour's snooze after our midday meal. He had settled down well and was happy enough lying on his rug at my feet, but I knew I had to harden my heart and start his training.

A sheep dog lives for his work of gathering together a farmer's flock of sheep on the moor, either to take them to a

116

new pasture or inspect them for one of the many afflictions that Dartmoor life can bring with it. He has no place as a pet, although once accustomed to living outside in the yard he can become a useful watchdog.

I told Boy all this as I fondled his black head, before getting up and taking him outside. Fly's kennel was just as he had left it, although I had burned his old rugs and bedding. Now I put Boy's fireside rug into it, fastened the dangling chain on to his collar and told him, 'Settle down, Boy, while I collect the eggs and make sure Ebenezer hasn't run out of water, and then we'll go and have your first lesson with the sheep.'

But he didn't agree with any of that. He strained to get free, and as I disappeared into the hen house I heard his heartbreaking howls — which suddenly stopped as I emerged with a basket of fresh eggs and saw Joe, on crutches, leaning against the kennel and stroking the puppy. Surprise and pleasure in equal measures hit me as I hurried over to him.

'Joe! How lovely to see you. However did you get up the hill? Come inside. You must be ready for a sit-down; I'll make a pot of tea.'

As we sipped our drinks, he told me his news. 'Leg's mending, missus — all that plaster stuff the hospital put on.' His wrinkled face grinned happily. 'And doses of my daughter Martha's herbs — good old knitbone for one. Now I'm feeling me old self. Vicar gave me a lift up here in his trap, and I shall walk down later — slow but sure with these old sticks!'

I poured a big mug of strong tea and, remembering his sweet tooth, stirred in three spoonfuls of sugar. 'Wonderful news, Joe, and I'm really glad to see you again. So what do you do all day, now you're home?'

He chewed on a slice of moist gingerbread before replying. 'Well, I sees to the garden and helps Biddy where I can, but mostly I sits and wishes I were working again.' He looked at me wistfully. 'Any chance of you having me back at Larkhill, missus? I hear as you'm working yourself too hard, what with the baking and all.'

I thought how good it would be if he could throw off his crutches and resume all the hard work he was so used to doing. But I knew it was impossible. 'I'm sorry, Joe,' I said gently. 'Of course I'd love to have you back here, but . . . '

We looked at each other and he sighed. 'No, course not. Jest a dream, missus. I'll 'ave to stay home and try not to get under Biddy's feet.'

Boy started howling again, and I knew I must get on with the next job that awaited. I refilled Joe's mug and offered him a bit more gingerbread. 'I'm sorry, Joe; I must start training that dog. But you can stay here as long as you like. And I hope you'll take that walk down the hill slowly. Be careful, won't you?'

He nodded, and I left him by the fire,

wishing old broken legs could mend more easily and that dreams might come true. But the afternoon sun and its glorious warmth, together with the beauty of the landscape, put healing hands on my restless mind as Boy and I climbed up through rough moorland to find my flock of sheep.

This time Boy had no fear when the ram headed up to him and stamped its feet. Instead, he lay down and growled and fixed it with his eye — the familiar expression that working dogs share. I knew he wasn't ready yet to have complete freedom, so I made sure I had some tidbits in my pocket with which to lure him back to me after his first run with the sheep.

He ran out behind them, and suddenly there was that characteristic pose of lying down and waiting for instructions. I whistled, something I had done all my life and which was useful now. I taught him the sounds for *go right*, *go left*, and *lie down*, and he seemed to understand them very quickly. Yes, there were the makings of a really good sheepdog in Boy. He came back when I waved a bit of fried liver in the air and grinned at me as he ate it.

But then something went wrong. As I bent to attach the leash to his collar, ready to return home, he jumped back and ran. And ran . . .

'Boy! Boy, come here! Boy, Boy . . . ' My voice rang out over the moorland and the green fields that sloped down to the village, but Boy ignored the calls.

Cursing to myself for not having watched him for that last minute, I hurried back, thinking he might well have run home. I got within sight of Larkhill, out of breath, wishing my legs were a bit stronger, and ready for a sit-down by the fire. But before I reached the entrance to the farmyard, I saw Mrs. Yeo from the cottage next door standing at her gate with a length of rope in her hand — and on the end of it a panting Boy, also worn out from his wild free running.

'My word, Lucy,' she said, frowning,

'you shouldn't have let him off like that — untrained dogs don't come to no good round here, and well you know it; farmers worried 'bout their sheep are quick to use their guns.'

I caught my breath, pulling it deep into my chest and feeling strength return. 'I know that, Mrs. Yeo. He just got away from me. Thank goodness he had the sense to come home. Good of you to catch him for me.'

Her frown died, but she kept her hand on Boy's rope. 'No trouble, me dear. But goodness, you looks tired. Come on inside and let me brew you a cup. You could do with a rest, I reckon.'

I wanted to say no — there was the baking to finish ready for tomorrow — but Mrs. Yeo put her free hand on my arm and smiled at me. 'Jest ten minutes, dearie. 'Twill do you good. Cos from all I hears, you bin working too hard, what with poor ol' Joe an' his broken leg. That lad Mike might be doin' what he can, but it's not enough. Seems to me you needs another man

122

about the place.'

I let out all my breath and was about to argue with her, but weariness overwhelmed me. The idea of a few minutes resting by someone else's fire, and drinking tea which I hadn't had to make, made me just nod my head. 'All right, Mrs. Yeo,' I said weakly, 'I'd love to come in, thanks very much. I'll just put Boy in his kennel first.'

She handed me the rope and watched while I took the dog into Larkhill's yard and settled him in the kennel. 'And don't you dare start howling,' I said sharply before returning to her gate.

Dear Mrs. Yeo, always such a good neighbour, was kindly offering me exactly what I needed at this moment — ten minutes' complete rest. I went into her homely little kitchen and sank into the sagging armchair in front of the crackling fire. *Bliss*, I thought, and felt my strength begin to return.

10

Sitting there in the quiet warmth and sipping our tea, Mrs. Yeo and I looked at each other and smiled. The minutes stretched past and then, as my strength returned, I felt my heart start to beat a little faster as my thoughts grew, and it came to me that I had something to ask her. Slowly, nervously, I found the words.

'You're right, another man about the place would be just what's needed. And Stephen Neal has offered to help with the farm work. But, you see, I can't have him at Larkhill, because . . . because . . .' I came to a stop and was thankful to see understanding spread over her lined face.

'Course not, lover, not with all the gossips doin' their evil whisperin'.' She paused and I saw the thought surface in her mind. The smile returned as she broke the short silence, saying simply,

'Why, I can give him a room, if that's what you'm askin'. Always empty, it is, young Jeb's room, since he went up north to work.' The smile grew wider. 'An' folks won't talk 'bout an ol' woman like me takin' in a lodger, will they?'

I shut my eyes, feeling tears threatening. How wonderful it would be to have Stephen next door, working every day with Mike and releasing me from the increasing burden of overwork. And Apollo could share the stables with Duchess and graze with my cattle up on the moor, as he had done recently. I felt my heart beating more slowly, my eyes widening and a sense of happiness stealing through me. I leaned forward and clasped her hands.

'Thank you, oh, thank you,' I whispered. 'It would solve so many problems. Dear Mrs. Yeo, I can't tell you how grateful I am.'

She returned the pressure of my hands and nodded. 'I can guess, lover — but now it's up to you to fix it all up with Stephen. I expect you know where he is, do you?'

My heart began to sink. No. I had no idea where he might have gone after being turned out of Hayes Farm by that crosspatch, Emma. Well, I would have to find out — and soon.

* * *

The afternoon passed without any idea of where to find him. I was very busy, what with the yard duties and the baking necessary for Lizzie's basket next morning. When she arrived in the morning, she had news for me.

'My goodness, Emma's bin making her cake, so I hear, and it went soggy in the middle! And o' course, she's crosser than cross, and sayin' as how your ol' book was all wrong. But I think Will would've told her off for sayin' that. And as I come up here I saw Mrs. Rudge with her black bag walkin' into Hayes Farm, so I reckon the baby's comin' soon.'

I put the last gingerbread man on top of the new Victoria jam sponge cake and looked at Lizzie, wide-eyed. 'How did you hear all that?'

Her lovely grin faded. 'Went into the shop, see, cos Alan's been being nasty 'bout me coming up here. Says he needs me in the shop more. Anyway, there was all this chatter going on. But he told all the ol' dears to get on and go home.' She looked at me with an earnest expression. 'You know, Lucy, I think Alan is planning something to try and stop you selling your cakes. He don't smile so much now.' She sighed, shook her head, picked up the full basket and headed for the farm entrance. But before she reached the lane outside, she turned and called back to me, standing in the kitchen doorway.

'Nearly forgot — heard one of the ol' gels talkin' bout someone — a tramp or a beggar, don't know — livin' in Mr. Forester's old ruined barn. Wondered if it might be Stephen. Why don't you go and look?' When she saw my horrified expression, she added quickly, 'Course, it's probably not him.'

I went back into the kitchen without answering, but my thoughts were running riot. Why should she think I ought to know? Was I responsible for Stephen? Did everyone in the village still think there was something between us?

I rolled out some pastry too heavily and threw two mutton pies into the oven, knowing it was too hot and the tops would burn, but I was too worried to think straight. Boy fussed around my feet, and I knew I must put him in the kennel after a quick run around the orchard while the pies cooked. I shouted at him when he tried to jump the hedge and get away from me, and when I chained him up again I saw disappointment all over his little face, and hated myself for being unkind. Which, of course, ended in me feeling a fool, being soft over a dog. I chastised myself, knowing I must pull myself together and get on. When the pies were ready — yes, they had brown, crunchy tops but were still edible — I sat down and thought more sensibly.

Mrs. Yeo was expecting me to find Stephen and pass on her invitation to lodge in her spare room. That would mean I could ask him to work on Larkhill Farm until he found a new home. So I must go and find him. After Mike had finished his midday meal and set off with Boy on a leash up over the moorland to see to the cattle, I set out to find Mr. Forester's old barn.

It wasn't far away, just over the bridge and on the boundary of the village: a tall, neglected building with ivy and brambles growing over its once thick thatch, now hanging in wisps of dying reed from the dusty eaves. As I neared it, walking through the overgrown field, I smelled wood smoke and saw a small stick pile leaning against one of its falling-down walls. So Lizzie and the village gossips were right — someone was living here. Mr.

Forester was a semi-invalid and spent most of the year abroad. So unless someone in the village reported whoever had made it a temporary home, there would be no trouble.

I tried to shore up my positive thoughts as I stopped at the open doorway, not knowing what to do or say. And then I saw, just inside the barn, a jacket I recognised: an old woolen coat with patched sleeves and a loose pocket. It hung untidily on the back of a broken chair, but it told me all I needed to know. Stephen was here.

As I stood, wondering what to do next, a familiar, deep, vibrant voice sounded behind me and I turned round, feeling my heart race and colour rush into my cheeks.

'Lucy?' He came from behind the barn, carrying a bundle of green stuff, and stopped at my side.

'Stephen!'

We smiled at each other, and I felt a deep sense of something like love spreading through me. It wasn't the old childhood mixture of fondness and occasional anger, but something warmer and more important. Unable to control these feelings, I simply held out both hands. 'Thank goodness I've found you!'

He was very close, taking my hands into his and looking deep into my eyes. 'That's the nicest thing you've ever said to me, maid. I wonder what it means?'

The question made my smile grow even wider. He sounded as glad to see me as I was to see him. 'It means I have good news for you,' I said a bit unsteadily, my voice amused and quiet. 'Mrs. Yeo, my next-door neighbour, is offering you her son's empty room until you find your own home. And I'm asking if you really meant it when you offered to help at Larkhill. Because if so . . . '

I stopped abruptly because his great peals of laughter were echoing around us. He held on to my hands and said lightly, 'And what does it cost you to make all these offers, Lucy? The maid who said she didn't need a man to help her out?'

But I was lost — the warmth of his voice, his laughter, his blue eyes the colour of a summer sky, and his closeness. I just shook my head, finding no sensible reply, and then he put his arms around me and we held each other and kissed. For what seemed an endless moment, time stood still. Then, even as we breathlessly let go of each other, I heard a horse nickering and was instantly catapulted back into ordinary life. Apollo came around the corner of the barn, elegantly stepping up to Stephen and pushing his velvet nose towards the pocket of his jacket.

Stephen took hold of the bridle and stroked that curious nose. 'Sorry, boy,' he said, 'I've run out of sugar and carrots, so you'll have to do with something else.' He grinned as he bent to pick up the bundle of greenery that had dropped to the ground as we had embraced, and offered Apollo some leaves on the palm of his hand. The horse snorted, stepped back, and I imagined I saw disgust in the intelligent dark eyes. At once my mind was back at Larkhill, and I suggested to Stephen that he graze the stallion with my cattle until he found a likely home in which to establish his stud. My magical moment had gone, vanishing behind a cloud of everyday life and the work that awaited me back in the farmhouse and its yard.

I watched Stephen feeding Apollo the leaves; then, taking in a deep breath, I walked away from him until I stood at the entrance to the field. There was a last moment of lingering regret; a pain of wondering what might have been, if only I were able to change my life. But as Stephen watched me walk into the lane and latch the gate behind me, I felt the old, sensible Lucy reassert herself.

'I'll tell Mrs. Yeo to expect you any time, Stephen. And I'll be glad if you can help Mike, as the sheep need regular looking over, and I'm too busy with my baking to do it.'

I waited for an answer, but all he did was nod his head and say, 'Tomorrow.

I'll be there tomorrow.' Then he let me go.

I walked briskly up the road, crossing the bridge and taking the road to Larkhill. I didn't turn to wave, but I felt his eyes on me as I left him.

Larkhill awaited me, empty and quiet, and I went into the kitchen, pushing away all the raging confusion that had tormented me as I walked home. I tended the fire, pushed the kettle over the leaping flames and made a pot of tea; always a comfort. Then I sat down and drank it, trying to come to terms with what had just happened. First of all, I remembered what Lizzie had said. I supposed she would obey her brother, and stop helping me. But if so, how could I go on selling my cakes and pies?

And there was this sudden acknowledgement of my true feelings about Stephen. I smiled rather painfully: I supposed I had always loved him. Now he would be here, working on the farm. Even if he spent his evenings and nights with Mrs. Yeo, he would still be too near. Too close. Too important in my life.

I got up in a hurry, busying my mind with what I must do next: baking, and telling Mike that he would at last have help. And of course I must tell Mrs. Yeo that her kind offer had been accepted. I left the house and walked towards her cottage, telling myself that the kiss between Stephen and me had just been another making-up business after a few short, sharp words last week. Just another common or garden embrace, as used to happen between rough, arguing children. What a welcome thought. And I clung to it.

11

Mrs. Yeo nodded her head when I said that Stephen would very much like to take her offer of a room, at least until he found the farm he was looking for. I added that he would graze his stallion with my cattle, and that he would help Mike with the farm work. I looked at the floor while I said all this, wondering what her reaction would be. I let the silence continue until I raised my eyes and saw her looking at me, considering, as if she had something she needed to say but wasn't sure how to.

Slowly, and choosing her words with obvious care, she said, 'I think you'm working too hard, Lucy, my lover. Getting thinner, losing some of your lovely colour. 'Tis all that baking. It's too much for you, and you bin worrying over the farm work, I know.'

We looked at each other. I gave a stiff

smile and said with a weak sort of laugh, 'I'm young and hale and hearty, Mrs. Yeo. I shall last for a few more years, I think!'

'Course you will, my lover. But 'twouldn't do not to have some help. Like I bin thinking, I could help you with some of the work. After all, though I'm an old gel, I have time to spare. And I could come in and help a bit; like clearing up the pans and things, and even help mixing when you got a lot to do.'

Again our eyes locked. But this time mine were widening, and my smile was real. 'Mrs. Yeo,' I said quietly, 'how good you are. And yes, of course I should love to have you in with me, though I don't want to make you work too hard and get too tired.'

She gave me a big smile. 'That's decided then,' she said firmly. 'An' don't worry about me getting tired. I'll be along tomorrow morning, d'recly young Stephen's come up to arrange 'bout the room.'

I relaxed, had another mug of tea,

told her about using Ma's recipes and how Emma had borrowed the old book, then got up and went back to Larkhill. I felt something warm and lovely inside me; a sort of certainty that things were improving.

When Eli came to collect his birthday cake, I was pleased to see his smile as he took the big box and handed over a few shillings. 'I hope the little one will like it,' I said. 'It was a pleasure to make it for your family. Tell your friends, perhaps, and then I shall be able to make some more.'

He grinned at me as he put the box under his arm. 'Doing well, are you, missus? That's good. And don't take no notice of what ol' Alan Hannaford keeps telling everyone — that you'm bakin' bad stuff up here. Might give anyone food poisoning, so he ses!'

I waved goodbye to him and went back to the flour-lined table, thinking about what he had said. Was Alan so grumpy because I had turned down his advances? What should I do about it?

★　★　★

So the days passed. I accepted that Stephen was next door; and although I had to speak to him to outline the work that was needed, I said it in as few words as possible, without looking at him too directly. After a bit I told myself that my life was taking a more positive path. Of course I was still worried about Alan and his nasty warnings to everyone, and also the fact that Lizzie had said she had to stop selling my wares every morning, as her brother was forcing her to do more work for him. So the basket outside the gate was no more, and I had to take down my lovely notice. But Mrs. Yeo was good company for an hour each day.

Early one morning, Boy's barking sent me to the kitchen door and I found Stephen standing there, looking at me severely. 'Can I come in, Lucy? I think we need to talk,' he said without that usual smile.

What on earth could this be about? And why didn't he smile? A terrible thought hit me — had something happened to my cattle, my sheep?

'Yes, of course. Come in, Stephen,' I said, and pushed forward the cane chair for him to sit in. But he stood up in front of the fire and nodded at me to sit down.

'Don't look so worried, maid — all's well with your stock,' he said, giving me a hint of that familiar smile. 'It's you I want to talk about.'

'Oh,' I said as I tried to calm my mind.

He pushed the kettle onto the range and turned and reached for the teapot on the mantel. 'Us'll have a mug of tea, shall us, maid?' he said with the old grin, and at once I felt better.

I sat up straighter and said a bit tartly, 'Yes, of course. But for goodness sake, Stephen, sit down yourself. I can't put up with you looking down at me like this!'

The grin grew bigger. He pulled a

140

stool out from under the table and lowered himself onto it. 'All right, missus. Gotta do what you'm tellin' me as I'm working fer 'ee now.'

We both laughed, and at once the atmosphere grew lighter. With mugs of tea and a slice of treacle tart each, we sat there and looked at each other.

'Well come on then, out with it,' I said lightly. 'What do you want to say?'

He nodded, put his empty mug on the table, stretched his legs out to the fire and put his hands together on his lap. 'I want to tell you that you're working too hard, Lucy, and I have a good idea that will be a lot of help — if you'll allow yourself to think about it.'

I felt a flicker of uneasiness. I remembered Stephen's ideas as being positive, but sometimes a bit odd. And this one involved me. 'All right,' I said shortly, 'tell me then. But don't expect me to agree with it, will you?'

He didn't answer at once, but looked at me, and I saw a laugh in his eyes. When he did speak, his voice was low and warm. 'Lucy, I know you for what you are, and it's because of that I'm daring to make this suggestion.'

'Well, what is it?' I heard a childish peevishness in my voice, but I watched his face and saw the expression lighten, and at once felt less anxious. Stephen would never ask too much of me.

'It's about your baking, maid. Mrs. Yeo and I have been talking about it, you see, and she tells me that Lizzie Hannaford can no longer do the selling for you up here, outside your gate. But I think the village has realised by now that your goods are excellent. So we thought a bit, and I came up with the idea that you should start a tea shop up here. You would continue selling your cakes and pies and the like, but in a better and much more attractive place.' He stopped and looked at me.

My heart fluttered. A tea shop? Here, at Larkhill? Where on earth would it come from? Did he propose building it for me? And what would the village think? All sorts of doubts ran around my mind, but I saw him smiling at me and amusement spreading all over his face, and knew he understood just what I was thinking.

Slowly, I calmed down. I took a very deep breath and tried to get all my worries into one sensible question. Various answers slid into my thoughts; the village would love a tea shop, and surely no one really believed everything that Alan Hannaford was saying, did they? People would come, I was sure of it. Look how they had already stumped up the hill to buy out of Lizzie's basket. And they would be so curious. Then it came to me — dear old Joe could find a place in a nice new tea shop, and perhaps Mrs. Yeo would also help out.

In fact before I said anything, I knew in my heart that this was a wonderful suggestion and I wanted it to happen. Slowly I gathered my senses, met those direct blue eyes, and said loudly and firmly, 'I think that's an amazing idea, Stephen. I have no notion of how I shall manage to build a new tea shop — but yes, I want to do it.'

I saw him smile — one of those big, all-encompassing smiles that lit his face and made his eyes glow — and felt an identical smile lighting my own face. I sat there and let my imagination take hold. A tea shop, my baking, lots of visitors . . .

His voice broke abruptly into my dreams. 'I thought we would do it together, maid. You've got lots of old sheds out there in the yard, none of them used now; we'll choose the best and I'll get down to it. We'll make it into something that the village will admire — a place that's good to come to, filled with your wonderful cakes and pies.'

'And treacle tarts, and biscuits, scones, seedy cake, and, and . . . ' I sat back in my chair and started laughing. This couldn't be happening, could it?

Stephen leaned across the hearth and took one of my hands. 'Come out into the yard, maid. We must decide which shed would be the best choice. Then we can start planning, and I'll get down to the work in the evenings. Come on, up you get.'

He pulled me to my feet. Out in the yard, with Boy jumping around our feet, we surveyed the derelict buildings.

Something was also jumping around inside me, and after a few seconds I realised it was excitement together with a tiny bit of pleasure. Stephen was beside me. We had a plan to share and work to be done between us. Surely I could allow myself to enjoy the moment?

We looked at one knockabout old shed after another. They all looked quite useless, dirty and falling down, and slowly my excitement began to disappear. I stared into the interior of the biggest one, which used to be my father's workshop, and memories flashed through my mind. Pa had spent his few hours of relaxation out here, making things for Ma to use in the house: a fire guard for when we were all out of the house, shutters for the north-east window to keep out the winter gales, even toys for

Pete and me. Where had that little railway train gone that had been such a wonderful Christmas present long ago? I wondered.

I stiffened my back, took a great breath, and turned to look at Stephen. 'I don't think any of them will turn into a tea shop,' I said bleakly.

I watched him as he went into the old workshop, looking about him and even fingering some of the beams and the window frames. He came back to my side and his eyes fixed on mine. 'If you want something badly enough, you can usually get it, maid,' he said gently. 'Yes, none of these old ruins offer much hope; but look around this one and try and imagine it repaired, the beams supported, windows clean and frames stronger, and surely you can see how it could come to life, can't you? Tables, chairs, pretty curtains, and all your cakes and pastries on plates on a huge table at the back there, waiting for your eager customers to order. Can't you see it, Lucy? Try, maid.'

146

His hands were holding mine again, warm and compelling in their strength. I looked away from those mesmerising eyes and stared about me. And yes, of course I could see it — a tea shop here at Larkhill, a place to gather, a place that would maybe help make the village community friendlier perhaps. I felt my face relax and a smile spread across it. I looked down at Stephen's hands around mine, and the thought came like a ray of sunshine on a dull day — Stephen would do this for me. And I was happy to share it all with him. Pleasure flooded through me and, as all the gossip and nasty words and suggestions swept away, I flung my arms around his neck.

'It's going to be marvellous!' I cried. 'Oh, Stephen, when can you start, and what can I do to help?'

He held me for just a few seconds and then carefully stepped away. His smile was a big one, his eyes laughing, but his voice was low and controlled. 'Quieten down, maid, or you'll have the tea shop talked about down in the village before I've had a chance to start. Just remember, all this rebuilding and so on has to be fitted in with the farm work.'

That warning helped me, indeed, to quieten down. I remembered the sheep and the cattle, and Apollo up there on the moor, grazing; hens' eggs to collect and clean ready for market; Ebenezer to see to; feed to measure out; peat to bring in for the fire; and an evening meal to make for all of us.

I turned away and walked soberly back to the farmhouse, went into the kitchen and tried to think what job to do first.

12

Eli came three mornings later, a big grin on his leathery face. 'Missus Neal, she's got her baby — bouncing baby girl, she is. Will ses she's over the moon — baby's good, don't cry too much, but the missus is worryin' 'bout her ol' cake. Hers went soggy, see, and Will ses I should ask you if you can make her another — a proper one.'

'Goodness!' I was surprised, but pleased too. So the baby had come safely, and Emma wanted a good cake. Well, I would certainly make one.

I took the post Eli offered and said, 'When you go to Hayes Farm tomorrow, tell Will that I'm making a cake for Emma, and I'll bring it round in a day or so.'

Eli nodded, stepped back from the doorway, looked around the yard and then asked, 'Where's the dog, then? Not run off, has he?'

'No.' My smile faded. 'He goes out with Mike and Stephen every day. They're training him to work with the sheep.'

'Oh, ar.' Eli continued on his way but I stayed where I was, looking at the empty kennel and feeling a little prod of resentment that Stephen had taken Boy from me. Yes I had agreed that Boy needed training, and yes it would be sensible if he went with Stephen every morning.

But I was mistress of Larkhill by rights; I should have been the one to do the training. I didn't have the time, though, did I?

I sighed and looked down the yard to the shed that was being worked on every evening. The tea shop was slowly taking shape: the dirt and general mess had been swept out, the beams were supported, and last night Stephen and Mike had worked on the window frames. Stephen had said he would go into Moreton this afternoon and get some glass cut to the right size for the actual window. Because he had probably seen the less-than-happy look on my face, he had stopped and said jokily, 'Nearly time for you to go and buy the curtain material, maid — decided what pattern you want, have you?'

I had mumbled something silly, and his smile had died. He had turned back into the shed, and I hadn't seen him again during the evening.

Now I stood there, looking around; not just at the yard, with all its waiting work, but at Dartmoor, spread out all around me. Huge, gleaming tors catching the sunlight. Moorland, wild and unmanageable, stretching in every direction. My homeland. It struck me that I was being petty-minded, letting small things distract my purpose in life — which, surely, was to make the best of all I had. And here was this new tea shop, with all its exciting possibilities, that Stephen was making for me. I walked into it and stood looking at every small detail, wondering at the skill and hard work that were turning it into something new and lovely. Then I went back to the kitchen, my smile replacing the dull thoughts.

When Stephen and Mike came in for their midday meal I greeted them brightly. 'Good news!' I said, dishing up some turnip and bacon pottage and giving them each a big slice of freshly baked bread to soak up the gravy. 'Postman Eli says that Emma has had her baby — a boy! And Will wants me to make a cake for him. I'll be doing that this afternoon. I wonder what she'd like? I wish I had Ma's old book — I expect there's a recipe specially for marking the arrival of a new baby — but Emma borrowed the book and I haven't had it back yet. Oh well, I'll just have to make one up.'

Stephen took a big spoonful of pottage and then looked at me. 'I'll go over to Hayes this evening,' he said. 'Must congratulate the proud father.' His grin made me smile. 'And maybe I'll get your book back for you, maid.'

I wondered if he and Will could be

making up. That would be good. I offered another spoonful of pottage, and he nodded with a big grin.

★　★　★

I thought very hard, wishing again that I had a big store of recipes to choose from, and then decided just to make a big fruitcake that the Neal family could cut into and enjoy over a few days. Luckily I had dried fruit and nuts and a tiny cup of brandy to make it special, and when it came out of the oven later that afternoon I was pleased with the result — good, round and firm, and smelling rich and lovely. I thought Emma would be pleased; and it struck me that if Will and Stephen were making friends again after all their rows, then so could Emma and I.

Next day Eli brought me a letter from Tavistock — a note from Annie to say that she and Pete were hoping to call at Larkhill on Sunday afternoon and please be sure to be in. I knew I must have a good tea to offer them. So, more baking! I was up to my arms in flour, making treacle tarts, when a knock at the door made me reach for a cloth to wipe myself tidy. And who should be there, smiling at me, but Mrs. Greening, the vicar's wife.

I invited her in, saw her seated comfortably beside the fire, then pulled the tea caddy down from the mantel. We talked briefly about the weather — good for the coming corn harvest — and Emma's new baby.

As I poured her a cup of tea, she cleared her throat. 'Lucy, your idea of having a tea shop here at Larkhill is all around the village. People are talking about it wherever I go. Which is why I'm here.'

Surprised, I offered her some shortbread biscuits and then sat down opposite her, wondering what this could be about.

She went on, 'You see, my dear, the vicar and I are very worried about the gossip that runs through the village

— and some of it particularly naming you.'

'Yes, Mrs. Greening?' I felt anxious — had the gossip got worse since Stephen moved in next door?

She must have understood my feelings, for she smiled and put out her hand to touch mine reassuringly. 'Now then, I didn't mean to worry you, Lucy. We have thought about this problem and, well, it's your tea shop that has filled our minds, my dear! Such a wonderful thing to do — and I'm sure the village is very excited. You see, we hope that once it's open it will bring people up here, and we believe that all their gossip will be forgotten as a new sense of village community takes its place.'

I stared at her as pictures flashed through my mind: my tea shop, a possible meeting place for all the villagers who had a little time to spare and fancied a freshly baked cake and a nice cup of tea. And there might even be holiday-makers during the summer, people who had never been to Dartmoor and were exploring the villages. This could be helpful to all the old ladies in their lonely cottages who would offer bed and breakfast. Goodness! I saw it all happening — and all because of Stephen's wonderful idea.

My eyes were shining and my smile was wide as I said happily, 'Oh, Mrs. Greening, it all sounds so wonderful — do you think it will really happen?'

She finished her piece of shortbread and looked at me with a kind expression. 'If you make up your mind and act accordingly, Lucy, wonderful things can always happen. I know you are strong-willed and very active, so I'm quite sure the tea shop will be opening before the end of the summer. And the vicar will be willing to bless it, if that's what you would like.'

I was lost in dreams of smiling people eating my cakes and tarts, of old Joe and Mrs. Yeo helping out, and people being friendly to each other instead of exchanging unkind gossip; so for the moment I didn't answer. And of course Stephen was there in my mind — Stephen, who had offered me this excellent dream that I could see coming true.

I resurfaced from my thoughts and saw that Mrs. Greening was looking at me, waiting for my reply. 'That would be very kind of him — and yes, I would love him to come up and bless my tea shop, Mrs. Greening.'

She rose, adjusted her hat, and pulled on the gloves that had lain in her lap while she ate the shortbread. 'I will give him your message, Lucy, and hope that your tea shop may be open before Widecombe fair, when we could advertise it. The corn harvest will be in, and people will be ready for some new interests. September is only a month away, so perhaps we can arrange the blessing for, let's see . . . the eleventh, I think. Let me know how things go, won't you, and I will put the date in the vicar's diary.'

Together we walked towards the open doorway, where Mrs. Greening stopped, looked at me and smiled. 'I hope this tea shop will bring you happiness, Lucy, my dear, for I feel you deserve it. Well, goodbye now; I must hurry back to the vicarage. So much to do, you see.'

The pony waiting in the gig whinnied, and then she was up in the driving seat, flapping the reins and giving me a last wave as she drove the gig out of the yard and down the hill. I stood there watching until she was gone, then slowly and thoughtfully returned to the kitchen and the baking that awaited me there.

That afternoon I packed up Emma's fruitcake, tied up the box with my old hair ribbon to make it look pretty and important, and set off walking down the hill to Hayes Farm. Stephen and Mike hadn't come home for a midday meal, but had taken a basket of bait with them up onto the moor where they were working with the sheep, so I'd had no news from Stephen, who had visited the farm the evening before to congratulate Emma and Will. I told myself he would probably come and see me later in the day. I hoped so.

Hayes Farm was busy. Will was in the yard seeing to various things; and Emma's mother, Mrs. Hardcastle, who had come for the birth, was fussing around in the kitchen preparing the next feed. She looked at me with small, dark eyes and a face that clearly found it difficult to smile at strangers. I asked how mother and baby were.

'Doing well,' she said briefly. 'I s'pose you want to see them, like everybody else in the village, eh?'

I was a bit taken aback; if Emma's mother was like this, it certainly went some way to explaining why Emma herself wasn't more friendly. But I smiled back. 'If it isn't inconvenient, of course I'd like to see them.'

She nodded, looking as if I'd asked the biggest possible favour. 'Come on then,' she said with a sigh. 'And don't stay too long. The lass had a bad time and she's tired.'

'I won't — I just want to see her and

the baby and give her this cake.'

'Cake?' She was leading me out of the kitchen and up the stairs, looking over her shoulder at the box I carried. 'Emma don't have a sweet tooth. But it'll come in useful, I daresay, for when we have the christening party.'

I can't say I was pleased with this unfriendly reception; but when we reached Emma's bedroom and I saw her, pillowed up in her four-poster bed in which I supposed generations of Neals had been born, I was glad I had come. She smiled such a smile at me, one that I wouldn't have believed could belong to that crosspatch, Emma.

'Hallo, Lucy,' she said and waved a hand at her mother hovering behind me. 'Find a chair for Lucy, will you, Mother? And let her see Russell.'

I went quickly to the cot standing beside the bed and looked down at a tiny, wrinkled red face that suddenly opened its mouth and let out a wail. I bent down, put out my hand, and felt his own minute hand grip my fingers.

And something happened inside me. This little scrap, making so plain its needs and wants, was Russell Neal, who would, God willing, one day grow into a huge man in charge of the family farm. Russell, new and small as he was, was touching a nerve inside me, suggesting something amazing and unbelievable. That something remained, growing bigger and more important, even as I turned back to the bed and sat in the chair produced by Mrs. Hardcastle and tried to think what to say to Emma, who looked as if she had become someone new; someone who smiled as she put out her hand to stroke her son's hairless head.

She said in a warmer voice than I had ever known, 'How good of you to come, Lucy. I'm so pleased to see you.'

I had no words, so just smiled back and put the box of cake on the bed beside her. But inside me that feeling still glowed.

13

That evening Stephen and Mike hurried through their meal because they wanted to get on with the remaining work in the shed. My visit to Emma and Russell had made me thoughtful and quiet.

'Anything you want to say about the work we're doing, Lucy?' said Stephen as he pushed back his chair.

I looked at him, saw his smile was missing, and suddenly realised I wasn't being any help. I pulled myself together, pushed away the image of that tiny baby in his cot, and concentrated instead on my surroundings. I followed Stephen to the door and then pulled his arm so that he turned and looked at me.

'I'm sorry,' I said in a low voice. 'I want to talk to you about the tea shop. You see, the village is getting excited, and I'm being offered lots of help. Could you come in later so that we can talk about it all?'

He nodded, looked at my hand on his arm, and slowly smiled at me. 'Of course, maid. Yes, there's a lot of things to discuss. I'll be with you before bedtime.'

I felt a gradual uplifting of my pensive mood, knowing now that between us we could sort out all the various ideas that were running around my head. Between washing the dishes and waiting for him to come in, I made a list of things I needed to share with him. For instance, where would we find tables and chairs for the tea shop? There was a small table in the spare bedroom upstairs that would do for one, I supposed, but no chair to go with it. And then tablecloths — I pictured them, white if possible, or perhaps brightly checked ones; and napkins to go with them. And then all the crockery. I made up my mind not to use mugs but to splash out on nice china, with perhaps a flower on the front. I had some money in savings, so I could go into Munster's in Moreton and order a couple of china tea sets.

Suddenly, the enormity of the undertaking hit me. A tea shop, up here, in the Larkhill yard! Would people bother to walk up the hill just for a cup of tea and a cake or biscuit? Was it foolish of me to expect the idea to be successful? By the time Stephen came in, took off his jacket, ran a hand through his dusty hair and looked at me, I was almost determined to tell him to stop work on the shed because I'd had second thoughts. The idea was clearly ridiculous and would never work. But there was something in his smile and in his quiet, deep voice as he led me to the fireplace and almost pushed me into the cane chair before sitting down opposite me and stretching his legs out to the hearth.

'Everything's going well, maid,' he said, and I heard warmth and reassurance in his words. 'We'll get there soon, and you'll be delighted with the finished little room, I promise you.'

How could I not cheer up then? I pushed my list across the table and watched his face as he read it. 'Quite a few demands, Lucy! It's good that you've thought them all through. Well, I can tell you one thing to cross off already. I've an oak table that Will is offering you — the one we did our lessons around a long time ago. It's round and big; it'll hold all the cakes and pastries you're offering. It'll look good.' He paused, then went on, 'I haven't had time to tell you about my visit to Hayes Farm last night, have I?'

My problems faded away. Stephen nodded when I asked if a mug of ale would go down nicely as he talked. I placed it by his elbow as he began telling me how he and Will had sat down in the barn because his mother-in-law, Mrs. Hardcastle, didn't like untidy men sitting about in her kitchen. I caught his eye then and muttered a few words of my own, which he smiled at, before telling me how proud Will was of his tiny son.

'Seems like a new person, does Will — and all because of that baby,' he said. 'Extraordinary! But good. And we were able to patch up a few of the problems that have caused us to fall out since I came home. You say that Emma is different, too? I'm glad, for her quick temper wasn't easy for Will to deal with. Or me, for that matter.' He took a drink of the ale, put the mug back on the table, and sent me a look that showed he still had something to tell me.

'What else? There is something, isn't there?'

'Yes. I asked him if I could have your ma's recipe book, which you lent to Emma. He went to look for it, then came back and said she had let Alan Hannaford borrow it, as he said he needed some new recipes now he was making his own cakes.'

The expression of pleasant warmth on his face had disappeared and I felt uneasiness grow inside me. 'So,' I said sharply, 'I take it Alan hasn't returned it to Emma?'

Stephen's answer was short. 'No. So I'll have to go and get it from him when I have time.'

We looked at each other, and at once I recalled the argument the two men had had after the barn dance. I also remembered all that Alan had said to me, and how he had spread bad words about me through the village. I sighed and saw how Stephen's eyes narrowed as he looked across at me.

'Don't worry, maid. I'll get it back, and then there'll be no more unpleasantness. Now, shall we take another look at your list? What's next? Chairs. Hmmm, wonder if the vicar could spare some old ones from the village hall.'

At which point I realised I hadn't told him about Mrs. Greening's visit. We talked on until Boy, lying on my feet, whined to go out, and Stephen got up.

'Dark already, and I need my sleep.

I'll put Boy into his kennel.' He paused and looked down at me. 'All right, maid? No more worries?'

I smiled and shook my head. 'I think some good fairy might well come down and solve any other worries, Stephen. You have a way of magicking things and making them happen,' I said.

He paused beside my chair, and for a moment I thought he might lean down and touch me, perhaps even kiss me. But then he turned and walked towards the door.

'Magic?' he said, his voice strong and deep. 'Doesn't do to believe in such a thing, maid. Reality is all we have to work with.' He nodded at me, one hand on the door latch. 'I'll say goodnight now, and see you tomorrow. Come on, Boy. Bedtime.'

Then they were gone; just footsteps in the yard, a clank of the chain as Boy was tethered to his kennel, and silence. I sat on by the dying fire and went over all we had talked about until my eyes started to close, then doused the embers and took a candle to light my way to bed.

★ ★ ★

Next day, extraordinary things started to happen. Mrs. Yeo came in and offered me a beautifully embroidered linen tablecloth. 'My old auntie sewed this,' she said. 'Embroideries of all the flowers in her garden. I never use it now, and I thought it might be useful when the tea shop opens. Would you like to have it?'

I took it from her, opened it, spread it out over the table and gasped. Such wonderful colours — daisies, scabious roses and even tiny forget-me-nots all around the edges. What a piece of art! And yes, I could see it on the oak table Will was giving me, the basis of the big ornamental spread of all the cakes and biscuits and scones and pastries I would be offering my visitors. I looked at Mrs. Yeo and remembered the words I had spoken to Stephen last night: magic! Yes, this was a sort of magic, surely.

I put my arms around Mrs. Yeo and kissed her soft cheek. 'Thank you,' I said. 'This is a beautiful gift, and I'm so grateful. It will have pride of place and everybody will admire it!'

'Well,' she said with a little embarrassed laugh, 'you deserve the best, Lucy, maid, and I'm glad you're pleased. And I think my old auntie would be delighted to see it being shown off.'

We smiled at each other for a moment longer, and then she said briskly, 'Well, what can I do for you this morning? You said something about a chicken pie yesterday.'

We got to work then, stopping for a mug of tea once the pie was in the oven, and then I heard steps outside the door. I looked up and Lizzie came bouncing in.

'Hallo!' she cried. 'Just in time for a cup, am I? Good!'

I nodded at my empty chair and she sat down, grinning at Mrs. Yeo, who was clearing up the pastry board and the spilt flour. 'Well,' I said, pulling a stool from under the table and sitting down again, 'What's the news? Who's had babies, who's getting married, what new scandal is everybody talking about? Come on, I can't wait to hear!'

'Oh you're behind the times! Of course, Emma's had her baby — going to call him Russell, they are. Now there's a name for you.' Lizzie drank her tea, and then her eyes sparkled again as she looked at me across the rim. 'But *you're* the news, Lucy Wells! You and your famous tea shop that's going to put the village on the map and bring all the holiday-makers here!'

'Oh!' I didn't know what to say, so just stared at her bright face.

'And I've come to let you that Alan isn't at all pleased about the tea shop. He thinks it will go badly for his shop sales. And I tell you what, Lucy — he's turned cake-maker, trying to get back at you. But his cakes aren't a patch on yours, so you don't have to worry.'

I sat still, remembering what Stephen had said about my ma's recipe book. At last I said soberly, 'If he's making the recipes my ma made, then the cakes should be very good. But I don't suppose he knows much about baking, does he?'

'Nothing at all,' said Lizzie. 'Made Mrs. Harris a lardy cake and she said she fed it to the pig because it was so heavy!'

I joined in with her and Mrs. Yeo's laughter, but then added quietly, 'I want that book of recipes back, Lizzie. They're going to be the cakes and pies and things I make for the tea shop. Do you think you could get it for me?'

Lizzie's bright smile faded. She shook her head. 'I wouldn't dare ask, Lucy — he gets in such a temper these days.'

We looked at each other thoughtfully, then she added, 'But I suppose I could look around the shop and see where he keeps it, and take it without his knowing. I'll try, Lucy. I really will try and get it for you.'

'I don't want you to have any trouble with Alan, Lizzie. Leave things as they are. He'll probably give it back eventually.'

At that moment there was a rap on the door, and there stood Eli, grinning at us. 'No post today,' he said, 'but I got a message from Miss Stanley, who ses she's got two small tables she don't want, and would you like 'em? If so, tell me and she'll get the carter to bring 'em up the hill.'

I could have hugged him, but I didn't. Instead, I went and found a newly filled biscuit tin and gave it to him. 'Tell her yes, please, Eli. I'll go and see her this afternoon. And give these to your little ones. Thanks for coming all this way; it's so kind of you.'

Lizzie jumped up. 'Must get back,' she said. 'Eli, give me a lift on the bar of your bicycle, will you?'

'Well, I dunno,' he said doubtfully, but she was already out in the yard and he went after her, I imagined to make sure she didn't ride the machine and leave him to do the walking. I heard their voices as, with Lizzie perched on the bar, the old bicycle slowly took to the road.

Going back into the kitchen, I crossed my fingers and hoped all would be well with the journey. Mrs. Yeo smiled at me as she untied her apron and patted her wispy hair. 'She's a funny one, that Lizzie,' she said. 'But what a friend you got there, maid. They're a blessing, are friends like that, I'd say.'

I followed her to the open doorway. 'Yes,' I said, 'you're right. And it looks as if everyone has some sort of blessing for me today — you and Lizzie, and now Miss Stanley.'

We smiled at each other and I watched her go back to her own cottage, while I went indoors again and tried to decide which new made cake I would take to kind, grumpy old Miss Stanley that afternoon.

14

Miss Stanley was pottering in her tiny front garden when I arrived at the gate. She screwed up her eyes to see who I was. 'Lucy Wells!' she exclaimed in her frail, rather husky voice. 'How nice to see you. Come and sit down beside the rose bush. But first, just take this basket and put the weeds onto the pile of rubbish round by the side door, please. I've done enough weeding today, and my legs are aching.'

I did as she asked, then sat beside her on a creaky wooden bench in front of her living room window. I waited until she had fidgeted herself into a comfortable position.

'Miss Stanley, postman Eli gave me your message this morning, and I've come to talk to you about it.'

She looked at me and frowned. 'No need to talk about my getting rid of a couple of old tables. All I need is a yes or a no.'

I knew Miss Stanley of old; she had been our school teacher, and we had all sat quietly, trying to remember what we had been ordered to learn. I met her deep-set, rheumy eyes and smiled warmly. 'The answer is yes, Miss Stanley, and thank you very much. Actually, your offer has come at just the right time, as the tea shop I'm opening in Larkhill farmyard very soon is in need of furniture. So your two tables will enable me to offer tea to more villagers, once they've walked up the hill to find me.'

'Yes, I heard someone in the village talking about this tea shop — but it was only when the postman told me that I understood it was you, Lucy Wells. Good gracious! What would your parents have said, I wonder?'

'I think — I hope — they would be pleased, Miss Stanley. I'm finding it hard to work the farm alone now that Pete is married and gone away, but so many people are offering me their help that I believe it would be a good venture.'

'You haven't married, have you? A pity. When you're old and alone you'll find you'll regret not doing so. Hard then to find much to be happy about, let me tell you.' She half-turned, the better to really look at me, and then added, 'Not too late, perhaps. You're a good-looking maid — a bit tall and strong, but then that's farming for you. Got anyone in mind, have you?'

I nearly fell off the bench. What a thing to say! But that was typical Miss Stanley. I stayed where I was, laughed a bit, and had the pleasure of seeing her face crack into a half-smile.

'Forgive me,' she said. 'Always said what I thought — and it doesn't always work.'

'No,' I agreed. 'I'm the same. But at least we understand each other. And as for marriage, well . . . ' I stopped and pushed away my dreams. 'I'm biding my time, so can't say one way or the other.'

We both laughed again, and I knew I must change the subject. 'I know you prefer plain things like the seedy cake my mother used to make. I believe she gave one to a school party once, which you enjoyed. So I've made one for you; it's in my basket. Shall I take it inside?'

With a great effort she pushed herself off the bench and walked very slowly to her open door. 'Come in,' she said, and I followed, putting the cloth-wrapped cake on her table. I watched as she shuffled into the scullery, beckoning to me as she did so. 'There they are, Lucy. Yours if you want them.'

They were two small, round bamboo tables that had an early Victorian look about them. At once I could envisage them in the tea shop, each with its small vase of fresh flowers and a plate of newly baked scones, a dish of cream, and some homemade raspberry jam. They were elegant, big enough for two people to sit around, and exactly what my tea shop needed.

'Thank you,' I said. 'And I hope that

you'll come to my tea shop and sit around one of these, because I want you to see how useful your gift is.'

'The carter will bring them to Larkhill next week, Lucy. And yes, I will most certainly come and visit you in your tea shop.'

I realised my visit was ending, so I took my basket and walked into the garden, looking back as I said my goodbyes. 'Thank you once again, Miss Stanley. And enjoy the seedy cake. Goodbye for now.'

Her small voice echoed my goodbye. I walked back into the village, then up the hill to the farm, thinking about all she had said — and pondering the possible truth of finding happiness hard to come by when I was old and still living alone.

*　*　*

It was almost time for Stephen and Mike to come home when Lizzie suddenly came panting up the hill.

'Can't stop, going to a meeting at the village hall — something to do with the fair next month — but I wanted to say that if you buy some linen I'll sew it into napkins for you, Lucy.'

'That's so kind of you, Lizzie. I'll be going into Moreton in the morning to buy curtaining; I'll drop a length of linen into the shop on my way back.'

As I watched her turn and start running down towards the village, I decided that when I was in the shop, I'd ask Alan myself about Ma's old book. Sitting by the fire, cooking vegetables for the evening meal, I wondered what might happen next when I did.

What a day it had been, with so many good friends offering help as they had. But now it was evening and I just wanted time to quieten down and realise my good fortune, and also to measure window frames so that I bought enough curtaining in the morning.

I was in the yard, coming out of the shed — no, it was the tea shop now! — when Mike came up the hill,

Duchess puffing a bit as she pulled the cart into the yard. Stephen followed, mounted on Apollo. I forgot measurements and stood there, thinking how grateful I was to both of them, putting in all that extra work just to give me a tea shop. Boy came bouncing up to me, and I made a fuss of him while Mike dealt with Duchess. Stephen waved as he led Apollo into the stables. 'Be with you in a minute, maid.'

I nodded, returned to the kitchen and pulled the pan of vegetables onto a cooler part of the hearth, to wait there until both men were ready for their meal. I wrote down the window measurements on my list, put it safely on the mantel ready for the morning visit to Moreton, and then sat down, thinking of all that I could tell Stephen about my lucky day. But as soon as he came into the kitchen, hands wet from the pump outside, and came close to the fire, smiling down at me, I saw something new in his face — an expression I hadn't seen before. Not exactly worry, but something I didn't like. I felt uneasiness grow inside me.

'Everything all right, Stephen? No problems with the stock today, I hope?'

He paused, then sat down opposite me. 'No problems, maid. Apollo's enjoying the grass, and your bullocks are keeping inside the walls. And Boy's learning fast. I've put him in his kennel with some water and a meal; he's earned a good supper, and then he'll rest.'

We looked at each other, but neither of us said anything. My nerves jangled, and all the excitement I had felt about sharing the news of the day died away. I got up, pushed the pan of vegetables over the flames again, and opened the oven door to see that the mutton pie was ready. Then Mike came in, so everything became different.

He and Stephen ate their meals with good appetites, and I heard about the sheep, the bullocks, and Boy's improvement, followed some banter between the two of them as Stephen teased Mike about his courting of Daisy, the miller's daughter. We might have been a small, happy family, I thought wistfully in the middle of my meal. But it wasn't so; I knew that as soon as the plates were emptied both men would go out to the tea shop and put in the finishing touches before going to their respective beds. And I would be alone, again. I had an inner strength now, though, knowing that the tea shop would soon open and I would have a new sort of life that would be more social and friendly than living alone in this old farmhouse.

I looked up at Stephen as he came towards the fireplace and saw again that strange expression. For a moment he stood there, and then he said, in a low, quiet voice, 'Lucy, I have something to tell you.'

I knew then that my feelings had been right. Something had happened. Into the silence growing between us, I managed to push one word. 'Yes?' I asked. Then I added, desperate to break the tense atmosphere, 'Sit down, Stephen, and tell me. I hope . . . ' I cleared my throat, trying to sound more cheerful than I felt. 'I hope it's not bad news?'

He sat down, legs out to the fire, hands locked on his lap, and I fidgeted uncomfortably. 'No,' he said deliberately. 'It's not bad news, maid, but good news. At least, for me and Apollo.'

I just stared at him.

'You see, Lucy, I've found the farm I've been looking for. An old farmhouse with pasture land, and rights for grazing for sheep. Exactly what I was looking for. So, yes, really good news, except that . . . ' He stopped, leaned forward and looked intently at my shocked face. 'Not so good for you, maid — because, of course, working my own farm, I can no longer spare you any of my time.'

I said nothing. Thoughts where whirling around my startled mind and I could only stare at him.

'Good thing Mike and I got your tea shop finished, isn't it? You've only got the final touches to add to it now, and then you'll be in business. Oh, and by the way, I met the vicar on the way home today and he said yes, he can find a few unwanted chairs. He'll bring them up tomorrow when he's on his visiting rounds. That's good, isn't it?'

'Yes,' I said faintly. Of course it was good — chairs and tables being kindly given to me, Lizzie making napkins, Mrs. Yeo offering to help in the tea shop, and possibly Joe finding a part to play now that he was walking more easily. But a black cloud had settled over all this excitement. I knew that I was going to miss Stephen more than I had ever thought possible.

He was sitting back in his chair, his smile warm as he watched me. 'Well,' he said, 'got something to say, surely, haven't you, maid? I thought you'd be pleased.'

Somehow I pulled myself together, knowing that I mustn't spoil his pleasure at having finally found what he wanted. I got up from my chair and forced my face into a smile as I crossed the room, going to the cupboard where half a small barrel of cider lived. 'Of course I'm pleased!' I said, pouring out two mugfuls and putting one on the table beside him. 'Let's drink to it! It's wonderful, Stephen, that you've finally got what you were hoping for. And where is this farm?'

I went back to my chair and drank some cider, hoping it would somehow banish the sadness I felt. I thought he looked relieved. Had he felt that I would miss him? Be lonely here, on my own again? But I refused to let these unhappy thoughts spoil the moment. I raised my mug and gave him the brightest smile I could summon up. 'Near here, is it?'

'It's Teignhead Farm. Out on the moor. I met the old boy who used to farm there at the market last week; told him I was looking for a place to rent, and he offered.' He gave a triumphant smile. 'I snapped it up at once. But I haven't told anyone except you, because I have to wait until all the papers are signed and my money paid. And once that's done, I can move in when I like, with Apollo. And so I can think about buying a mare and starting my stud.'

I heaved in a big, strengthening breath. Teignhead Farm was a bit far out on the moor, if I remembered correctly, but why should that worry Stephen? I was still looking at him, sipping the cider, when he leaned forward again, put out a hand and touched me.

'I want you to come out and see it, Lucy. How about riding out with me tomorrow afternoon? I can give Mike a hand in the morning and wait for you to come out at dinnertime. Say you'll come — please?'

The warmth of his touch on my arm glowed through me, and I put my mug of cider on the table as I reached out my other arm and put my hand on his. 'Of course I'll come, Stephen. I'd love to see where you're going to be.' I paused, my thoughts rushing ahead. 'Tell you what — I'll bring a picnic and we'll eat it when we get there. How about that?'

'Wonderful. I'll look forward to it.' Having drained the cider mug, he got to his feet, walked to the doorway and then looked back at me. The smile was in place again, and I congratulated myself on not having spoiled any of his pleasure.

'I'll see you around midday then. And I'll bring a couple of treacle tarts!'

I watched him leave the house and latched the door behind him. I heard him say a couple of words to Boy; then there was silence as he went back to Mrs. Yeo's cottage.

I didn't go to bed for some time; I was too busy with thoughts to be calm enough to sleep, and I didn't want to be restless with churning dreams. But when I finally got to bed I lay my head down on my pillow and slipped at once into drowsiness, images and voices disappearing. My last conscious thought was that, after all the blessings I had received during the day, here was yet another — the gift of sleep.

15

In the morning I drove the trap into Moreton, firmly putting out of my mind the idea of Stephen leaving the village, and Larkhill, and instead concentrated on my list of things to buy. Munster's china shop had just what I wanted — a china tea set decorated with small pansies all over the cups. I bought three sets, dreaming of the crowds of holiday-makers who would come to eat my cakes next summer. Then I visited the shop that sold furnishing materials. That was a bit more difficult to choose — so many patterns. I finally picked material with a cream background decorated with pale green swaths of what looked like clematis, with very light mauve delicate flowers that I thought would complement the vivid colour of the pansy tea cups and plates.

Pleased with my purchases, I drove the loaded trap back to the village. There was one more task to complete before returning to Larkhill and putting last-minute touches to the tea shop. I hitched Duchess to a post at the front of the shop and went in, intent on seeing Alan. He came out of the small office at the back of the shop, stared at me, and then came to my side.

'Well, how nice to see you, Lucy,' he said, smiling. 'I hear you've got a tea shop up at Larkhill now, so I suppose you've come to buy some of my cakes? Yours not selling so well, perhaps?'

Anger sparked inside me. How dare he be so patronising? 'Mine are selling extremely well, thank you, Alan, which is the reason I am opening the tea shop,' I said curtly. 'I've come this morning to ask you to return my mother's recipe book, which I believe Emma Neal lent you.' I didn't smile, but stared into his narrow dark eyes which, as I spoke, became even narrower.

'That's nonsense,' he said quickly, slipping a hand into his jacket pocket and leaning against the counter beside me. 'Never believe a word that Emma says! If she had the book, then she's probably lost it or given it away. I can't help you, I'm afraid, Lucy. But while you're here, perhaps we could arrange to step out together one evening?'

This was too much. My anger swelled, and I reached out my arm and pushed him. He almost fell sideways, which didn't improve the expression on his face.

'No, thank you, Alan,' I said sharply. 'I have no wish to go anywhere with you. And I must insist that you do have my mother's book.' I turned swiftly, pointing at a tray of cakes his assistant was putting into the window display. 'Because that simnel cake is definitely my mother's recipe. I would know it anywhere. So just find the book and hand it back to me at once, please, as I'm in a hurry. I have a lot to do, what with my tea shop opening next week.'

The words flowed out of me, and then I realised I had given a date for the opening without any thought. I discovered I was smiling. So near! Well, I would have to work harder than ever to get everything ready in time. I looked at Alan, saw the scowl on his face, and held out my hand. 'The book, please.'

'I told you, I haven't got it.'

'And I don't believe you.'

He stood there, looking at me with a sort of smirk on his face, as slowly he said, 'What with a farm to run, and now a tea shop business, you'll never manage, you know. You need a husband.'

I felt anger flame inside me, and my voice became sharp as I snapped, 'Well if I do, Alan, it definitely won't be you!'

We stood glaring at each other for nearly a minute, until a customer came up to him. 'Mr Hannaford, I wonder if I could ask you about . . . ' Alan broke his glare and turned away.

I left the shop. I would have to go to Hayes Farm and ask Emma if she had the book, but not right now. Honestly

— married to Alan! Slowly my anger faded, and instead I started to laugh.

I must get back to Larkhill, start in on my final preparations, and then do some baking. I had quite forgotten that Pete and Annie were coming for Sunday tea, so I must make sure I had something really good for them to eat. I was so looking forward to seeing them, and my smile flowered at the thought of our reunion.

Driving Duchess back up the hill, something far more urgent occurred to me — I must make a picnic ready to share with Stephen when we rode out to Teignhead in about half an hour's time!

★ ★ ★

I rode Duchess back out of the yard along the rough track to the fields, then on through moorland where the heather was beginning to show small purple buds. All around me was the wonderful wilderness that was Dartmoor, and I allowed Duchess to take her time, slowly climbing the hilly terrain. We came to a halt beyond the newtake walls, where I saw Stephen waiting with Apollo. He waved, smiling as I reached him.

'Give me the basket, maid. Apollo is younger than poor old Duchess. You're in good time — Mike is still up there by the tor, with the sheep and Boy. So we'll go on, shall we, down to Teignhead?'

'I'm looking forward to it,' I told him, returning his smile. 'And what a beautiful day — this sunshine, and a cloudless blue sky.' I felt my spirits rising.

Once mounted, he led me down into the valley beyond the tor and then up again, towards the far moor where Teignhead Farm was. How lovely that ride was. Stephen and I shared our memories of long-ago picnics and games; of swimming in the icy rivers; of him and Will and Pete fighting occasionally, with me shouting at them to stop; of high spirits exploding into anger that just as quickly died away, leaving us all friends as usual.

It was well past dinnertime when we got to the top of the ridge beyond which Teignhead Farm lay. We reined in the horses and looked down at the wild valley with the young river Teign running through the bottom of it. There, set above the small clapper bridge across the river, stood the farm.

'Sit on the bridge with our feet in the water and have our picnic, shall we?' Stephen's grin was easy and warm, and I laughed with delight at the suggestion. Yes, that's what we used to do. The horses were glad to able to graze now, and we put the basket between us as we sat on the cold granite stone bridge.

'Bread and some chicken legs,' I said. 'And a pot of last autumn's chutney to go with them. I didn't bring a drink — we've got enough water here if we're thirsty.'

'And what's for afters?'

'Can't you guess? Your favourite treacle tart, of course!'

We sat there and ate every crumb of the picnic, then he got up and went down to the river, filling the pot that the chutney had been in and bringing me a drink. It was icy cold, just as I remembered it.

I got up and looked at the old building standing some distance away, and suddenly all my hopes for Stephen's new farm drifted away. For Teignhead was not just old, but neglected; by the looks of it, no one had farmed here for years. Beside me, Stephen was quiet too, and I thought he must be sharing my thoughts. Together we walked into the walled yard with its sheds and ruined byres, looking around us, then halted at the broken-down door of the house. I couldn't read the expression on his face. Was it determination to make this a living farm, or disappointment at its state?

After a moment, we looked at each other. 'Can you live here, Stephen? This old house is almost as ruined as my shed was. Are you going to do another building job and make this your own home?'

I looked into his eyes and saw they

were cold, but fiercely sure of what he was thinking. He waited another moment or two; then, lifting his voice and sounding as sure and positive as I remembered him to be, he said, 'Of course I can improve it. And there's land — that's the most important part, Lucy. Apollo can have mates here, and his foals will eventually breed a new strain of stallion. It's my dream coming true.'

I didn't argue. Once Stephen had an idea, he would never go back on it. I sighed. So this was what must be. His new home would be out here, on this remote part of the moor, with not even a neighbouring farm for company. 'But Fernworthy Farm is at least two miles away, Stephen,' I said weakly. 'Won't you be lonely?'

His smile beamed out. 'I shall be too busy for that, maid. Now, let's go in and see what the old place is like.'

I wasn't impressed — damp walls, broken windows, and earth floors oozing mud and filth. But he saw things differently. 'Good old fireplace, look at it — I shall keep warm even when the snow comes once that's burning.'

After we'd been as far over the house as was possible, we went outside again and returned to the bridge, where the horses looked up and nickered a welcome to us. Stephen looked around as he held Duchess ready for me to mount. 'Gorse is growing well — all that yellow blossom and nutty smell. And you know what they say about that, maid?'

'When the gorse is flowering, that's kissing time,' I said without thinking — and then my smile faded. What had I said? But it was too late. Stephen stepped closer to me, held out his arms, and I went into them without any more thought. I felt his strength, his warmth, his smell, his heart beating beneath his shirt. And we were kissing — but only for a few seconds.

My brain started working then, warning me that this was foolish. We could never be together, me at Larkhill and him out here on the remote moor.

So I stepped away and pulled myself up into the saddle. 'Come on,' I said briskly, not looking down at his surprised face. 'If my tea shop is opening next Friday, I've still got a lot of work to do. I can't waste any more time.'

Perhaps he was as disappointed as I was, but he covered his feelings, turning at once and mounting Apollo. 'So why is Friday the opening day? How have you arranged that?'

Before I knew it, we were riding back towards Larkhill and I was telling him of my unpleasant scene with Alan Hannaford; except, of course, I didn't repeat what he had said about me needing a husband. When we reached the farm, Stephen asked if he could stable Apollo for the rest of the day, and I said yes. He took Duchess from me and said he would see to them both, leaving me time to get on with whatever I had to do.

'Thank you,' I said, feeling something cold had come between us; but perhaps that was what fate had decreed. He turned at the stable door and looked back at me as I walked towards the kitchen.

'Don't worry about that recipe book, Lucy,' he called. 'I'll fix Alan Hannaford and get it back for you. And this evening I'll put up the curtain fittings and make sure the floor is as clean as possible. Thanks for the picnic — the treacle tart was wonderful.'

Then he was gone, and I went into the kitchen and looked wretchedly at the fire that needed building up, and at the bundle of curtain material, and all those china cups and saucers. And wondered exactly what sort of life I had got myself into.

16

The next morning I had unexpected visitors. The vicar's gig drove into the yard and he came to the kitchen door, smiling. 'Here are your chairs, Lucy. A little bit spoilt, I fear, but perhaps your lad Mike can remedy that? And they could do with a coat of paint, so I brought half a can I found in the garden shed.' The smile widened across his long, lined face as he added, 'And Mrs. Greening said you would need a good brush, so she found one. It's with the paint.'

I felt warmth run through me. 'Mr. Greening, it's so kind of you to do all this. I really am grateful.'

He unloaded the last chair, put the paint and the brush on it, and looked at me seriously. 'My dear, helping you is what we should all be doing — not just gossiping and saying unkind things. I hope other people have done what they can?'

'Indeed they have, Mr. Greening.' My answering smile grew wider. 'So many other people in the village are helping me. It's wonderful. I just hope they'll enjoy the tea shop as much as I intend to do.'

He nodded and looked at me with those perceptive eyes. 'You deserve to be helped, Lucy. Running a farm on your own must be hard for a single woman. I believe that Stephen Neal is helping you — until he finds his own farm, that is. What will you do when he can no longer work at Larkhill?'

This was the question that had hit me the moment I woke up that morning. What, indeed, would I do without Stephen's help? But Mr. Greening was still looking at me, and I knew I must find an answer. After a moment's pause I said, too brightly, 'I expect I shall find someone in the village who can give me a few hours. But first of all I've got to get the tea shop open, so I'm not worrying too much about that.'

Again he nodded. 'I hope you're right, my dear. Well, I must get on now. But Mrs. Greening and I shall be with you next Friday when your tea shop is ready to open.'

He climbed into the driving seat, clucked to the cob, and then drove out of the yard with a last wave to me.

Slowly I inspected the chairs. He had been right; they were all rather worn and dilapidated, but I knew Mike would be able to make them look as good as new — when he had time. That brought back the worry about help for the farm, but I pushed it away and went back into the kitchen, spreading the curtain material out on the table and finding a tape measure before cutting out two long curtains with wide hems.

I heard footsteps and a knock at the door, and Mrs. Yeo was looking at me with a big smile. 'So it's sewing this morning, is it, maid — no baking for a change? Here, let me pin those hems for you.' She sat up to the table, producing a pin cushion from her pocket, and doing all the fussy work which I found so difficult. 'Give me your sewing basket and I'll get on with them. You'll want to hang them today, I daresay? Well, I'll do my best, maid.'

I did as she asked and was delighted to see the speed with which she threaded the needle and, with tiny stitches about half the size I would have made, fashioned the cut-outs into proper curtains. But it was no good just standing there and watching her, so I turned my thoughts to making a special cake for Sunday teatime, for Pete and Annie's visit to Larkhill. If only I had Ma's recipe book . . . but there was no use dwelling on it. I put Alan out of my thoughts and decided to make Pete's favourite cake, a sponge filled with cream and homemade jam.

Halfway through the morning, footsteps sounded in the yard. Looking towards the door, I saw two people standing there — Biddy and Joe! I hurried towards them. 'Come in, come in! How lovely to see you both. And how did you get here? Joe, you didn't manage to climb that hill, did you? You must be so much better now!'

He grinned, pushing Biddy towards the chair near the fire, then leaning against the table where Mrs. Yeo was sewing the final curtain. 'Yes, missus,' he said cheerily. 'Got these old legs working again, and the hill wasn't too bad. We took our time, didn't we, Biddy?'

She looked up at him and smiled. 'Yes, indeed; all puffing and panting we were. But we're here now. And, Miss Lucy, we want to do something to help you with this tea shop you're opening. Just tell us what we can do. 'Twill be a pleasure, anything at all.'

I felt tears welling up in my eyes. How wonderful that Biddy and Joe, of all people, wanted to help out. I turned away, pulled the kettle closer over the hearth, and said a bit jerkily, 'Let's have a cup first, and then we'll think about work, shall we? Joe, pull that stool from under the table and sit down. You must be tired from that long walk.'

Mrs. Yeo talked happily enough to Biddy about village matters, and Joe muttered to me that he'd heard of a young man, new to the village, who might be looking for work, and maybe he could help out here at Larkhill if that's what I wanted. As I poured out four cups of dark, strong tea and pushed the milk jug around the table, I wondered if that was what I really wanted — a stranger here at Larkhill.

Slowly the talk died down, until Joe looked at me earnestly. 'Meant what we said, missus, we did, 'bout helping in the tea shop. Must be a couple of jobs us old folks can do?'

Thoughts rushed through my head. Mending the tables and painting them — Joe would be good at that, and now that his legs were stronger, surely it wouldn't tax him too much. And perhaps some shelves put up to hold the china. Tentatively, I asked him, and saw his face crack into a great smile.

'O' course I can do all that fer you, missus! No trouble. I'll go and look at they chairs right away.' He marched out of the kitchen to where Mr. Greening had offloaded his gifts.

Wonderful! I thought. And Biddy — ? Well of course, just the person to sort out the china on the finished shelves. I saw her watching Mrs. Yeo putting the last stitches into the curtains and, as if she felt my eyes on her, she looked at me and smiled.

'Well, Miss Lucy, and what's the job for me, then?'

'Would you consider being chief of all the china, Biddy? And storing it on the shelves Joe is going to make?'

She nodded her head. 'I'd love that, Miss Lucy. I'll go and have a look at they teacups, shall I? Reckon they'll need washing before you put them on the tables. I could get on with that, if you say so.'

Again, wonderful! I thanked her and showed her where the boxes of china were. Looking around me, I realised my kitchen was a hive of industry. Mrs. Yeo had finished the curtains and, with them gathered in her arms, got up to take them into the tea shop and put them there ready for Stephen, who had promised to put up the poles that evening. It would only be a small job for me to attach the hangers to the curtains and then they would be in place, decorating the small shed that had once been so wretched and ruined, and now looked so bright and welcoming.

As Joe and Biddy disappeared to start their individual jobs and Mrs. Yeo went off to the tea shop, I made Pete's sponge cake and then started in on shortbread and gingerbread, which would all keep ready for next Friday. But, of course, before my opening day there was Widecombe Fair on Tuesday, a day for all Dartmoor folk to meet up and have fun. Suddenly I knew I was eager to be part of it, so I made a seedy cake to enter in the cake competition. I wouldn't win, but it would tell all the villagers that I was a good baker, and that my tea shop would be worth visiting.

★　★　★

Joe and Biddy had done most of their jobs, promising to return tomorrow. They were walking slowly down the hill, having refused my offer of a ride in the trap, and Mrs. Yeo was back in her cottage. I sat by my fire, feeling mentally and physically tired. Indeed, it was only the thought of Stephen coming in to complete my window frames and hang the curtains that made me get up, smarten my work-soiled dress, tidy my hair, and put a smile on my face.

I was standing in the doorway, admiring the sunset and wondering if the bank of shadowy grey clouds meant a change in the weather, when the cart lumbered up the hill, Stephen driving and Mike beside him, with Boy leaping about in the back. Of course Apollo followed them, his leading rein held by Mike. It was so good to see them. I felt a change in my body and my thinking, for suddenly life seemed happier and brighter.

I greeted them and asked Mike to look at the vicar's chairs, which Joe had started to mend, then told Stephen to come inside where mutton and turnip pie baked in the oven, filling the room with appetising smells. Between them they untacked Duchess, took her into the stable with Apollo, and gave both horses drink and feed; only then did Stephen present himself at the pump in the yard and give himself a good wash, telling Mike to do so as well.

While I put vegetables on to cook, I heard them kicking their boots in the yard, trying to get clean enough to come indoors. Then they were beside me, sniffing the tantalising smells coming from the oven.

'There's some cider left in the barrel; help yourselves while I dish up, and come and sit down,' I told them. I looked across at Stephen and caught his eye. 'I have so much to tell you,' I said happily. 'It's been such a good day, you see.'

He came back to the table with his mug of cider, put it down and looked at me. 'I'm glad to hear it. Mine was not so good, but I'll tell you about it later.'

I heard a note of frustration in his deep voice, but decided that a good meal would do wonders to cheer him up. We sat around the table like a small family, Mike telling us his plans for going to the fair on Tuesday and how he hoped to meet Daisy there, while Stephen and I smiled at each other, glad to hear the boy sounding so happy.

'Stephen, what are your plans for Tuesday?' I asked as we ate the pie.

'I shall enter Apollo for the best stallion prize. And of course Emma is putting Russell into the handsomest baby competition — although Will tells me he might easily win the noisiest baby competition, if there was one.

Good lungs, he says.'

We all laughed, then I pushed the basket of apples into the centre of the table. 'No time to make a pudding,' I said breezily. 'And you know what they say about an apple a day!'

It was all very bright and comfortable. After Mike had left us to go and look at the vicar's chairs, Stephen and I remained sitting and nursing our mugs of tea. I knew this was a precious moment to remember, so that I always had something lovely to bring to mind when he was gone.

The sunset had finished flaunting its fiery colours, and now the evening dark had started to fall. I knew that very soon Stephen would go to the tea shop to do my curtain poles and hangers, but I wanted him to stay here, just him and me together, for a little longer. I told him about my visitors, and said how wonderful it was that people were being helpful and no longer gossiping about me.

He got up, looked down at me, and

said quietly, 'About us, you mean?'

I nodded, taken aback by his serious voice. 'Yes.'

'Well, I'll be gone next week, so there won't be any need for any more gossip. Though Teignhead is going to take far longer than I reckoned to make habitable again, so I shan't be settled as soon as I'd hoped.'

'Where will you live while you're doing all the work the old place needs?'

I watched his face become firm and determined. 'Out there, of course. Always a shelter to be found on the moor, and there are byres and sheds among the ruins at Teignhead. Apollo and I will find a warm spot.' He smiled and walked towards the door, pausing there to look back at me. 'Nothing for you to worry yourself about, maid. I'll go and hang your curtains for you now.'

He went through the door and I leaped to my feet. I couldn't let the evening end like this. I must show him how strong I was; how nothing mattered except running Larkhill and the new tea shop. 'I'd better come and see you do it right — men are so clumsy with curtains and things.' I heard the arrogance in my voice and knew he heard it, too.

He picked up the first pole, started stringing hangers on it, and then turned to look at me. 'Whatever you say, Lucy.'

Then he got on with the work while I just stood there and wished I could say something to make amends, but could find no words.

17

The curtains were up, hanging straight and beautiful, and lifting my spirits. I told Stephen to come back to the kitchen for a last mug of tea when he'd collected his tools, but he said no.

'Thanks, maid, but I need my sleep. I've got a lot to do tomorrow — I'm going to ride to Teignhead once I've looked at your bullocks. Mike can deal with the sheep, with Boy's help. So I'll say goodnight and be on my way next door.'

I nodded. What could I say? As I returned to the farmhouse I heard his boots scraping on the stony yard, going towards Mrs. Yeo's cottage. So I had a lonely mug of tea, leaving the pot on the range for Mike, who was still out with Daisy, and tried to cheer my feeling of loneliness by thinking of all that lay ahead, like Pete and Annie's visit on Sunday afternoon. What a lot of chatter we would have! That brought a smile. And on Tuesday I would join the rest of the village at Widecombe Fair. Stephen would be there with Apollo; the thought made my smile broaden. And then Friday I would be working hard in the tea shop, and in my kitchen once the Fair was over. How many cakes to make? Had I made enough scones? What about the clotted cream?

My thoughts kept me busy, chasing away the image of bleak old Teignhead Farm. I went up to bed feeling I had a good future, even if I was always alone.

* * *

Sunday came, and I was listening out for wheels and horse hooves from dinnertime onwards. Then there they were — Pete, as tanned as ever, smiling down at me as he drove the gig into the yard; and Annie, looking so pretty — and plumper. She ran into my arms once she dismounted. We looked at each other with huge smiles, and she nodded her confirmation to the question in my eyes. 'Yes, Lucy! I'm due in three months' time — isn't it marvelous?'

'Yes, oh yes, of course it is! Are you well, Annie?'

I had to keep words flowing, for suddenly my mind was in shock. My brother and little Annie, starting a family to grow up and eventually become part of the farm they were working. A legacy that was quite wonderful, but one I would never know. How I kept myself talking sensibly for the next half hour I shall never know. Luckily, Annie chattered away, telling me about the baby clothes she was knitting. Going out to the gig again, she returned with a small parcel. 'And of course we've heard about your tea shop, Lucy. You know how news spreads. It's going to be so successful, we're sure of it. I've knitted you a few tea cosies.'

Opening the small packet, I found

four beautifully knitted woolen tea cosies with — the surprise made me catch my breath — small images of pansies sewn into them. 'They match my tea cups!' I cried, and put my arms around Annie to thank her.

The afternoon passed too quickly. Pete said he must be back to help out with the milking, and they made ready to leave once the sponge cake had been eaten. I hugged Annie again, told her tenderly to take great care of herself, and felt tears welling behind my eyelids when she whispered, 'I want you to be the baby's godmother, Lucy. Will you?'

No words came to mind, so I hugged her again, closed my eyes and nodded. Finally, I was able to murmur, 'I shall be delighted to do so, Annie. And thank you for the honour.'

I watched the gig drive out of the yard and heard Pete's last words echoing in my mind: 'You say Larkhill is doing all right and you're managing, but you'll need a man, surely, once your tea shop is busy. I might just have someone in mind — a young chap wanting to move nearer to Widecombe. Let me know Lucy, how things go.'

I nodded and said, 'Thanks, Pete.' Then they drove down the hill, Annie turning to me with a last radiant smile before they disappeared.

* * *

Tuesday dawned a bit grey and windy, but with sun shafting down between the clouds, and it was time for Widecombe Fair. I drove Duchess in the trap and when I reached the green I was surrounded by other people, wagons and gigs, all making their way to the fields where sheep and cattle and ponies were being assembled. Children ran about shouting, dogs barked, and I felt happier than I had for many a long day. If only Stephen were here.

I left Duchess and the trap and walked around. I came across the tea tent, with steam coming out of its open flap, and guessed the tea urns were boiling away inside. Looking in, I saw lots of people sitting around a long table decked with cakes and biscuits. I thought Mrs. Yeo was probably there, perhaps even Miss Stanley. But nothing kept me in one place. I was waiting for Stephen to appear with Apollo.

Suddenly there they were, heading towards the last field where the stallion competition entrants were gathering. I ran to him, unable to control my pleasure at seeing him. 'Apollo looks wonderful! I'm sure you'll win, Stephen!'

He gave me a quizzical smile. 'Just hope the judges agree with you, maid. But look, I've got something for you; that's why I'm late getting here. Called in on Hannaford on my way.' He delved into his jacket pocket and produced my ma's recipe book.

I gasped as I took it from him. 'So Alan had it all the time. How did you make him give it back?'

Stephen's expression was tight and unfriendly. 'Let's just say he had the sense to go and find it in the end.'

'You mean — you had a fight? Oh, I do hope not.'

His smile was grim. 'It was waiting to happen. But don't worry about it, maid. And now I must get Apollo spruced up before the competition starts. Go and see your friends, Lucy; we'll meet up again later.' And he was off.

The book in my pocket felt as if it was burning a hole. I was so glad to have it back — but at the cost of Stephen and Alan fighting over it? I shook my head as I slowly walked out of the field and joined the laughing, chattering throng who crowded the green and the stalls set up all around. Yes, he was right — I should look for my friends and exchange my news and hopes with them. I told myself to be glad to be here. I was enjoying myself, chatting to old friends and laughing with Biddy and Joe, who were sitting in the tea tent and saying with twinkles in their eyes that the biscuits weren't as good as mine. Then someone came up behind me.

221

'Lucy, I have such good news for you!'

I turned and there was Lizzie, eyes wide and glowing, a great big grin on her pretty face.

'All right, let's walk down to the green and you can tell me all about it,' I said, smiling goodbye to Biddy and Joe, and following Lizzie as she marched outside. She was dressed, as usual, in a bright jacket, with a long pheasant feather in her dark hat. I thought how cheerful she always was and realised I was lucky to have such a good friend. What could be the news? I wondered.

I soon knew. She was bursting to tell me. 'It's Alan!' she began, dancing along beside me as we walked down through the crowds of people. 'I went to the shop to see if I could do anything, and he was there, grumpy and nursing a big bruise on his chin. Didn't say how he got it . . . '

Oh dear, I thought. But I couldn't help smiling. Lizzie was still going on.

'He told me he won't come here

today; he's arranged to be in Moreton, apparently, to walk out with the girl who serves in the bakery where he buys his bread. A nice, quiet girl, he said, who is no trouble to anyone.' She giggled. 'Not like you, maid! But that's good, isn't it? You don't have to think about Alan anymore, Lucy!'

Another voice sounded behind us and we turned. There was Emma Neal, all dressed up in a smart pale grey costume with a big dark red hat, carrying Russell in her arms. 'Hallo,' she said warmly. She was all smiles, and told us we should get ready for the cake competition in another big tent just down at the end of the green. So off we went, three smiling girls with a gurgling baby who seemed to be enjoying the fair as much as we were.

The tent was crowded, but we made our way to the front where we could look at all the beautiful cakes laid out on a big trestle table. 'There's mine, look!' Emma pointed at what I thought was probably a Dundee fruitcake, with the nuts and cherries sunk a bit into the middle.

But I said, 'Well done, Emma. Was that one of my ma's recipes?'

I saw her smile fade as she nodded. 'Yes, Lucy. And I'm so glad Alan's given you back the book — I kept telling him he must do so.'

Lizzie and I praised her cake, even though the top was a bit lopsided, and then Lizzie said, 'And there's yours, Lucy — that caraway seed cake over there. My word, it looks good!'

'Let's go and see if the stallion competition is under way, shall we?' I said, but Emma said she must find Will and let him take Russell so that she could roam the fair on her own for a short time. We watched her go, and Lizzie and I looked at each other and smiled at the change in Emma since having baby Russell.

Then we saw the stallions, their shiny hides looking wonderful in the brilliant sunshine and their long, spindly legs graceful as their owners carefully led them down the field to where the group of judges waited, eyes eagerly assessing each horse.

'There's Apollo.' I saw that Stephen had done a good job on the horse's gleaming coat. He must surely be the winner, so tall and well-behaved, though he gave a bit of a sidestep and a nicker as Stephen told him to stand still.

I felt my pulse start to race. Wouldn't it be wonderful if Apollo won the competition? I didn't know what the prize was, but it would help Stephen set up his eagerly awaited stud. Then Teignhead came into my mind — the money would definitely be needed if he was going to renovate the ancient farm.

It seemed an age while the four judges — gentry from our village and others around Widecombe, resplendent in their check jackets and bowler hats — inspected the entrants.

Lizzie became impatient. 'I can't stand still any longer. I'm off to the tea tent to have something warm and a slice of cake. If I don't see you again today, then I'll be at the tea shop early on Friday morning ready to help you with the opening, Lucy.'

She ran off; but I didn't mind being alone because Stephen was only a short distance away and knew I was here, watching and hoping.

How long they took, those judges! When we thought it was all over, they gathered in a tight little group in the corner of the field and talked and talked . . . I supposed they couldn't make up their minds as to the winner. Eventually though, all smiles, they walked back to the line of horses, and the chief judge, Mr. Benbow from Hobden Manor, put a badge on Apollo's bridle. 'The winner! Apollo, belonging to Stephen Neal. Congratulations, Stephen — and what a beauty you have here.'

There were handshakes, smiles and compliments all round. I stood back, watching as Stephen told Mr. Benbow all about his plans for starting a stud and Mr. Benbow nodded his approval. Then when everyone was moving away, Stephen came to me, and I stroked Apollo's nose.

'Well done, my beauty — how you deserve to win,' Stephen said. 'And now I hope you'll produce winning foals as well!'

I turned to him. 'And of course, it's all due to your love for him, and your care — so congratulations, Stephen! Perhaps we can go and have a cup of tea and a bun for a treat? I know everyone in the tea tent will be wanting to speak to you.'

He nodded. 'And then when it's all over and everything's quiet again, you and I must have a talk, maid. About your big day on Friday.'

I was about to answer when Will came up, holding a sleepy-looking Russell, and shook his brother's hand. 'Well done,' he said firmly. 'You hung onto the idea, didn't you, even though you had nowhere to live. Well I admire you, Stephen. And I hope we shan't have any more arguments.' Then he looked at me and smiled. 'And Emma got second prize for that cake of hers,' he said. 'She's really pleased, and ses it's all because of your ma's book.'

We laughed, a happy laugh that brought us together after all the differences of opinion and grey thoughts. Stephen grinned and said something foolish to Russell, and then we all walked out of the field, finding our way to the tea tent among the crowds ready to make their way home now the fair was over.

18

We talked, Stephen and I, when we got back to Larkhill. 'So now I have to get on with building my stud,' he said, lounging in front of the fire and smiling at me. 'Apollo has everything it takes to establish a good line, and by next year I hope to have a foal to enter at Widecombe Fair.'

I saw his face glowing with pleasure, all the ambition and determination in his wide eyes, and realised that this was just how I felt about Larkhill Farm, and about the tea shop. It suddenly came to me that we were two of a kind. So why must he live at Teignhead while I was here at Larkhill?

'Well done with the seedy cake prize, maid. Goodnight now, and I'll be here on Friday morning,' he said as he got up, stretched, put his arm around me, and then left to find his bed next door.

When he had gone, I faced the truth. All my loneliness and fears for the future were my own fault. I was proud and arrogant, thinking I knew everything about life, whereas in reality I knew very little.

I put Boy outside in his kennel and went to bed myself, my head full of strange thoughts. But I slept like a baby; and in the morning, despite the sudden bad weather, I knew what I was going to do — bake, of course. More cakes, lots of scones, some tarts and rock buns, a couple of fruit pies, and a final tray of gingerbread men.

For the last part of that busy day, I concentrated on the tea shop. With Mrs. Yeo at my side and Lizzie arriving at tea time saying she could spare me an hour, we laid our tables, each with a small vase of bright marigolds and moon daisies; stocked the shelves with all the fragrant, delicious-looking goodies; and then, exhausted, sat down by the fire, looked at each other, smiled broadly and drank mugs of strong, reviving tea.

'Saw old Joe as I came here,' Lizzie

said halfway through a shortbread biscuit, 'and he said the wind's changed — going to be wet tomorrow, but hopefully better on Friday. Have to keep our fingers crossed, won't we?'

I refilled the empty mugs. 'I can't believe it won't be a glorious, sunny day. After all, the vicar's coming, so I expect he'll arrange that!'

We laughed and I felt my remaining cares floating away with the smoke going up the chimney, because I had a feeling that all would be well. But a small voice inside me whispered that there was one more step to take, and I knew it told the truth.

Tomorrow, I thought, as I watched my good friends depart. 'See you on Friday, early — and let's hope the sun shines,' I said. But tomorrow was an even more important day.

★ ★ ★

It dawned grey and wet, with a storm from the south-west tearing at the grass and the trees, and making the river surge along with white waves. But the familiar Dartmoor weather was nothing to worry about. I talked to Mike and asked him to inspect the cattle, wherever they had found shelter, and then get Boy to gather the sheep in a corner of the field where the wind would no longer disturb them.

'I'll be back by dinner time I hope, Mike. Come in then and get dry and warm — and there'll be a pie in the oven if I'm a bit late. Help yourself.'

He looked at me curiously, pulling the sacking over his shoulders, his cap already pulled down over his eyes. 'Not going out in this rain, are you, missus? Anything I can do to help?'

'You're doing everything possible, and I'm so grateful,' I told him. Smiling and saying more than I meant to, I continued, 'Perhaps it won't be long before I get someone to take over half your work.'

He grinned. 'That'd be good, missus. Like Mr. Pete said on Sunday, p'raps that chap moving to Widecombe, eh?'

I laughed. 'Perhaps. We'll have to wait and see, won't we?'

As he marched off with Boy at his heels, I knew the time had come. I found my father's old coat, which was far too big for me but would deal with the rain, pulled my oldest winter beaver hat low over my face, and went out into the stables, where Duchess greeted me with a look that said, *We're not going out in this, are we?* But I made a fuss of her, gave her one of the carrots I had in my pocket, and said that this was to be a very important journey. So rain or no rain, we must simply get through it together.

With Duchess in harness, I put a basket containing a bowl of broth wrapped in hay to keep it warm beside me, and safely fastened some bread and cheese to the saddle. We left Larkhill yard, went up the rough track, and began riding slowly through the rain-drenched moorland.

It was hard facing that south-west

wild wind, feeling rain stinging what was visible of my face beneath the old hat. But Duchess and I plodded on, and I kept in my mind's eye what I would find at the end of this uncomfortable journey.

The ride to Teignhead Farm had never seemed so long, nor the landscape so threatening. No sunny, glinting tors, but hard stone frowning down at Duchess and me as we plodded along. The wind nearly took my hat with it, but I managed to pull it on safely. We reached the top of the ridge and, through the rain and the mist, I could just make out the lines of the old farm down in the valley. Warmth spread through me then, and I nudged Duchess into a sedate trot. We went down towards the river, which rushed along in such a hurry that I feared it would flood the small stone bridge above it. But somehow we got over it, and then it was only a short distance to the farm.

I dismounted and put Duchess in a ruined byre which had a bit of shelter, then made my way to the house. 'Stephen!' I shouted as I reached the door. 'Stephen, where are you?'

For a few seconds there was silence. Then steps sounded on the earthen floor and he stood there, staring at me with surprise written all over his face. 'What on earth are you doing here, Lucy? You came all this way, in this storm? You must be mad. Here, come in; I've got the fire going.'

He took my arm and led me into the far end of the house, where a fire burned patchily, swept by draughts and wind. But it was warm. He took off my wet coat, hung my hat on the back of a broken chair, and stood and looked at me. 'Well?' he said.

I read disapproval in his eyes, and I told myself to be brave. I had come on a mission, and now I must tell him exactly why I was here. I perched on the broken chair, held my cold hands out to the flickering flames, pulled in a huge breath, sat up very straight, and looked at him.

'Stephen, I've come to ask you to marry me.'

As I let my breath escape, I watched his face. Shock? Yes. Uncertainty? That too. But then slowly, I saw the familiar smile that made my heart jump with pleasure. A smile that mesmerised me, so that when he took my hands, pulled me to my feet and put his arms around me, I knew I was in heaven.

We kissed, and stood close to each other. His heartbeat echoed mine. His strength made me feel my own strength returning. And his joy brought my own out of hiding. We stepped apart, laughing, our faces echoing each other's radiant smiles.

'Well, maid, I thought you would never ask! But you surely know the answer? It's yes, yes, and yes again.' And then we laughed even louder.

The moment of delight gave way to thoughts, to dreams, to plans. I sat down again and he pulled up what was left of a hay bale on which he, too sat, by the fire.

'My beloved Lucy,' he said in that low, intense voice that sent shivers up my spine, 'are you sure this is what you want? A man living in your house, working your stock, giving orders? Even telling you, occasionally, what to do?' Here he chuckled, and I echoed it. 'It won't be the way you always said you wanted to live. I'll be there, too — yes, loving you, helping you, but finally becoming the man about your own home. Can you live with that?'

'I know now that I can't live without it, Stephen.'

No more words, just our eyes locking, sending messages that needed to be felt, not spoken. Until I remembered the broth and the bread and cheese. I stood up. 'I brought us a picnic; it's in the basket on Duchess's back, in that old byre.'

He got to his feet, arms reaching out for me. 'And what about the treacle tart?'

'I forgot it!' I said with mock dismay.

Laughter again, and then together we faced the wind and the rain, going to find Duchess and our picnic lunch out there in the relentless storm. We made our way into what was once a barn full of warm hay, which was now dark and empty save for a few bales that Stephen had brought into it to provide a rough sleeping place when he needed it.

'Not exactly luxurious,' he said as he pulled the hay into some sort of comfortable seating.

I sank down into it and opened the basket. The broth was still warm, and I had thought to bring spoons and a knife. Soup and bread and cheese, and Stephen and I sitting side by side, while the rain lashed against the closed door and the windows banged and whistled. But we were warm together. We were happy.

Once the picnic ended, Stephen told me that the next step was for him to go to the lawyer in Moreton who was preparing his contract for renting Teignhead Farm, and cancel it. We looked at each other, both knowing what would come next. He gently drew me down among the hay and looked into my eyes.

'I love you, maid,' he whispered.

I closed my eyes as I whispered back, 'And I love you Stephen — oh so much.'

We were together. We were going to marry. Everything was wonderful.

Later, when Duchess and Apollo were nickering to each other, demanding attention, we stopped our pleasure and got to our feet.

'Must get back to Larkhill. There's a pie in the oven — hope it won't be burnt,' I said, and Stephen nodded. 'Or perhaps Mike has eaten it all. Come on then, let's get ready for the long, wet ride home.'

As we mounted our horses and slowly climbed the valley hill, heading for the village and Larkhill, I repeated the word to myself, hearing it spread down all through my body, warming it, promising it all the things I had wanted but had pushed away from me. Larkhill would be our home, mine and Stephen's.

19

Mike came downstairs next morning, hiding something behind his back. He grinned at me, looking embarrassed, and produced a small white board on which the words WELCOME TO LUCY'S TEA SHOP were painted in large, beautiful black letters.

'Me an' Daisy wanted to give you something towards today, missus,' he said, 'so us did this. Hope you like it.'

I took the board, realised that it was exactly the one thing I had forgotten to organise, and then hugged him. 'It's lovely, Mike, thank you. And please thank Daisy for me. How good it will look on the gate. Will you go and put it up for me after you've had your breakfast?'

He nodded, looking even more embarrassed, and sat down. 'I'll do it, missus,' he said and rapidly tucked into his porridge. I gave him an extra spoonful of sugar in his mug of tea.

'No work this morning, Mike — leave the stock until after dinner; they'll be all right until then, I'm sure. I want you and Daisy to be with me for the tea shop opening. Thank goodness the weather has cheered up.'

Once breakfast was over, I went out into the yard and saw Stephen and Joe already in the tea shop. Joe waved and Stephen came to my side, smiling as he dropped a quick kiss on my forehead. 'My dreams were sweet last night, maid — and I hope yours were, too.'

'They were, Stephen. Such wonderful dreams. But now we have to get to work — and look at this sunshine! Just the weather to persuade the villagers to climb our hill and come to see what we're up to. I wonder when the first visitor will arrive.'

'No use just wondering,' he said with a grin. 'Go in and get all those kettles boiling, maid, while Joe and I set out the chairs. Biddy's on her way up, Joe said, and she'll get out the china and help Mrs. Yeo. No time for anything else.' He slipped an arm around my waist and drew me close so that I felt the warmth of his body and saw the emotion in his radiant eyes. 'Time for us later on. Much later.'

And so the first day of my new tea shop was upon us.

Back in the kitchen I filled four big kettles and soon heard them humming. Then Lizzie arrived, full of laughter, and kissed me as she wished me good luck. Boy was reluctantly persuaded to sit quietly in his kennel, chained up.

'Later on we'll give you a good run, me and Stephen,' I told him. And still later, I thought, we would make plans for our wedding.

Voices and footsteps sounded in the yard; Boy was barking; laughter rang out; familiar faces peered in at the open doorway; words reached me as I brewed tea and put fresh scones into the oven.

'Good to be here, Lucy. Hope it all goes well.'

'How lovely your little tables look

— can we sit down and order something?'

Lizzie and I greeted our friends, trying to remember their various orders, while Biddy calmly put cakes and biscuits, tarts and shortbread onto the pretty plates and set them on the trays spread all over the kitchen table. Mrs. Yeo was making pots of tea, and dear old Joe was carrying trays without spilling anything, chatting to his village friends as he did so.

I glimpsed familiar faces as I went into the tea shop to oversee things: Miss Stanley, of all people; Eli's wife and small daughter, telling me how lovely the birthday cake was; villagers who had known me as a child, here to see what I was up to; and Mr. and Mrs. Greening. Voices quietened as the vicar was recognised, but he smiled broadly and went around the tables, chatting to everyone, with Mrs. Greening following him. The happy hum of voices resumed, and I found Mr. Greening walking towards me, with Stephen joining him, while

Lizzie watched wide-eyed from the back of the room.

The vicar rapped his knuckles on the back of a chair, and all heads turned to look at him. Then he took my hand and looked at me with a warm smile. 'How good it is to be here with you all, in this new little part of our village. A part which I am sure will prove of benefit not only to hard-working Lucy, and Stephen and Mike, but also to the village. I'm sure holiday-makers will find it just the place to seek out as they explore our countryside. So let us all give a big hand to the clever, determined people who created this tea shop, and let our good wishes help them to continue building their new little business.'

He drew me towards him, kissed me on both cheeks, then turned to Stephen and shook his hand. I saw Mike hiding at the back of the tea shop and smiled to myself. At least he had heard his name mentioned.

And so the Larkhill Tea Shop came into being on that beautiful, sunny

August day — the day Stephen and I will never forget, for it was the day Stephen drew Mr. Greening aside after his little speech and said quietly, 'Lucy and I want to get married, Vicar. Can we come and see you and make plans?'

I saw great happiness spread across Mr. Greening's face and heard enormous warmth in his voice as he said, making sure that I, too, heard him, 'I shall be delighted, Stephen, and I think the village will be too. Come tomorrow evening, boy, and we'll arrange it all.'

As the vicar and his wife waved, smiled and left us, a gig drew up in the yard and out climbed Emma and Will, with a rush basket in which Russell slept. Stephen and I went to meet them and Emma kissed me, pointed at the baby and said mischievously, 'He didn't win Best Baby, not this year — but I'll enter him again next year when he'll be even more beautiful. Now, can we sit down and have one of your lovely scones with cream and jam?'

As I hurried back to the kitchen to

make sure the scones were cooked and ready to put on plates, I thought how wonderfully well the morning was going. Even better than I had hoped for. And I realised with great joy that all my problems seemed to be resolving themselves. Family arguments would be no more now, or so I hoped. Best of all, Larkhill would have a master again, to stand alongside its mistress. No more worrying about getting all the work done; no fears of seeing the old farm slide away into ruin and emptiness like poor old Teignhead Farm. And Stephen and I would be together.

Happiness ran through me; and then I remembered the scones, taking them out of the oven just in time. Another minute and they would have burned — and what would Emma have said then?

When it was all over, the last smiling villagers wishing us well and disappearing down the hill to their own cottages, Stephen and I stood in the empty yard, watching the sun go down. Such a wonderful day.

He turned to me and kissed me. 'Time for this busy day to end, maid, don't you think?'

I looked into those brilliant eyes regarding me with such love. 'Yes, Stephen. Let's go indoors.'

Together we went into Larkhill kitchen, and I bolted the door behind us.

We do hope that you have enjoyed
reading this large print book.

Did you know that all of our titles
are available for purchase?

We publish a wide range of high
quality large print books including:
Romances, Mysteries, Classics
General Fiction
Non Fiction and Westerns

Special interest titles available in
large print are:
The Little Oxford Dictionary
Music Book, Song Book
Hymn Book, Service Book

Also available from us courtesy of
Oxford University Press:
Young Readers' Dictionary
(large print edition)
Young Readers' Thesaurus
(large print edition)

For further information or a free
brochure, please contact us at:
Ulverscroft Large Print Books Ltd.,
The Green, Bradgate Road, Anstey,
Leicester, LE7 7FU, England.
Tel: (00 44) **0116 236 4325**
Fax: (00 44) **0116 234 0205**

THE PARADISE ROOM

Sheila Spencer-Smith

The stone hut on the cliffs holds special memories for Nicole, who once spent so many happy hours within its walls — so when she has the chance to purchase it, she is ecstatic. Then the past catches up with her when Connor, the itinerant artist she fell in love with all those years ago, reappears in her life. But has his success changed him? And what of Daniel, the charismatic sculptor she has recently met? Nicole's heart finds itself torn between past and present . . .

Other titles in the
Linford Romance Library:

STORM CHASER

Paula Williams

When Caitlin Mulryan graduates from university and returns to Stargate, the small Dorset village where she grew up, she is dismayed to find that the longstanding feud between her family and the Kingtons is as fierce as ever. Soon her twin brother is hunted down in his boat *Storm Chaser* by his bitter enemy, with tragedy in their wake — and Caitlin can only blame herself for her foolish actions. So falling in love with handsome Yorkshireman Nick Thorne is the last thing on her mind . . .